Hadji Murat

Hadji Murat

Leo Tolstoy

Translated by Hugh Aplin

ET REMOTISSIMA PROPE

100 PAGES

100 PAGES
Published by Hesperus Press Limited
4 Rickett Street, London sw6 1ru
www.hesperuspress.com

First published in Russian in 1912.
This translation first published by Hesperus Press Limited, 2003

Introduction and English language translation © Hugh Aplin, 2003
Foreword © Colm Tóibín, 2003

Designed and typeset by Fraser Muggeridge
Printed in the United Arab Emirates by Oriental Press

isbn: 1-84391-033-0

CONTENTS

FOREWORD

In all Tolstoy's fiction there is a tension between his need to preach and his prodigious talents as a storyteller and scene-setter. Increasingly, as he grew older, he was concerned with the great stained soul of his own country, interested in matters of religion and reform. Thus his skills at establishing the complexity of a single character through subtle and inspired use of detail and nuanced shades of feeling seemed, especially after the completion of *Anna Karenina* in 1877, to come second to his need to change the world. His short novels and stories written between then and his death in 1910 appear like beautiful moments of pure forgetfulness, times when his own great restless spirit was distracted and he managed to allow his political and religious preoccupations to play against the glittering constructs of his imagination.

There were times in the last thirty years of his life that his very hatred for authority caused him to tell a story which would place the authority in disrepute. In his fury he could work fast. *After the Ball* was written in one day in 1903. It told a story of great tenderness and cruelty, as a young man, in love with a colonel's daughter, experiences a night of rapture at a ball full of luxury and civilisation. And then at dawn he witnesses the colonel, who a few hours earlier has been dancing, mercilessly overseeing a prisoner being savagely beaten as he runs the gauntlet.

Hadji Murat was written in the same period and was Tolstoy's last major piece of fiction to be completed. In the year before his death his wife wrote in her diary, 'I have done nothing but copy out *Hadji Murat*. It's so good! I simply couldn't tear myself away from it.' It was not published until 1912.

Although Tolstoy used his own experiences as a young soldier in the story – he, too, lost money at gambling, as does Butler – he also did a good deal of research, reading memoirs and military histories and pestering his cousin, who knew life at Court, for information about Nicholas I. 'I absolutely must find the key to him,' he wrote in 1903. 'That is why I am collecting information, reading everything that relates to his life and personality. Mostly what I need are details of his daily life, what are called the anecdotes of history.'

He saw his warlord hero trapped between two despots. 'It is not only Hadji Murat and his tragic end that interest me,' he wrote. 'I am fascinated by the parallel between two main figures pitted against each other: Shamil and Nicholas I. They represent two poles of absolutism – Asiatic and European.'

This fascination, however, belonged merely to Tolstoy's genius as a polemicist and public figure; his real fascination was with the complex and untidy and unpredictable life which lay between the two poles. As an artist, he loved the pull of opposites within a character; he loved characters behaving out of character; and he also loved establishing a poetic moment in his fiction, a shimmering ending to a scene, for example, whose point was to create mystery and strangeness, because these interested his deeper nature more than any set of patterns or parallels.

In the opening pages of the story, we learn in ways which are beautifully concrete and memorable that Hadji Murat commands love and respect and loyalty. Soon, we watch the mixture of care and courtesy with which he moves. Having surrendered, he can be charming and beguiling, and then suddenly turn watchful and serious, stubborn and proud. He has become as mercurial and interesting as his author who also, in the years when he invented this warlord, was caught between degrees of disloyalty to the Tsar and the Tsar's enemies.

The spirit which guided Tolstoy's imagination was, at times, immensely tender. He wrote with sympathy and perception here about love and grief, finding it impossible to pass over a scene without allowing a background character a moment of yearning, or without insisting on offering a dramatic background to his minor figures. Neither could he resist drawing a portrait of the military which showed the officers awash with petty jealousy and boastfulness. And while Hadji Murat's story is one of loyalty and bravery in the face of treachery, the Tsar, Nicholas I, is merely venal and lecherous and obsessed with his own greatness. The pleasure which Tolstoy must have felt at depicting the infidel warlord as full of love for his family and the Tsar as one-dimensional and moody and cruel is palpable.

Tolstoy's Nicholas I in *Hadji Murat* is a feline creature whose arbitrary cruelties equal his vanity. Entering into his mind, coldly observing the obsequiousness of life at his Court, and balancing this against the death of an ordinary soldier or Hadji Murat's surrender, give the story the aura of a compass needle as it seeks to pinpoint Russia with its despotic ruler and its long-suffering population. Tolstoy, the fearless old preacher in his rural exile, must have written the court scenes with relish. In Chapter 17, when the villagers return to find their homes in ruins, you can feel his blind rage all the more strongly because he has introduced the villagers earlier in the story as though they were merely a small, placid stage on Hadji Murat's road to surrender.

His rage and his relish give way, however, to an extraordinary sympathy for Hadji Murat which has nothing to do with preaching or politics, and everything to do with the sheer range and power of Tolstoy's imagination. The scene where Hadji Murat gets ready to depart in order to rescue his family, for example, is one of pure emotion. The tug of memory and fierce attachment, the vision of his mother as young and handsome, and his son dressed and armed when he had last seen him, are set against the song of the nightingale and the noise of preparation.

Tolstoy's empathy is at its softest when he dramatises one of his central preoccupations – the innocent love of a young man for another man's wife. Early in *Hadji Murat*, Poltoratsky feels this love for Maria Vasilyevna, just as towards the end Butler feels it for Maria Dmitriyevna. This is part of the general patterning of the story in sets of doubles: the strange echoes between the fate of Sado's son and the threats to Hadji Murat's son, for example; or Nicholas I and Shamil, the despots who both order executions and experience similar uneasy feelings of lust, who exude power and pride, but whose self-delusion is almost matched with concealed guilt and self-reproach.

Hadji Murat himself stands against doubleness and patterning. Too headstrong and human, too proud and brave, too foolhardy and defenceless, too ready to let love dominate his plans, he towers above all those around him, fierce and independent. At the end, after the great quietness of the preparations for departure, just as Tolstoy has distracted us with thoughts of love, his hero's bloody and gruesome end comes as a shock. In his description of the last battle, which was also his own last description, the old master's essential genius – the art of making us see as though we were a witness – comes into its own with a pathos and majesty and pure excitement worthy of his great career.

– Colm Tóibín, 2003

INTRODUCTION

The majority of the characters who appear on the pages of this last major work of fiction by one of Russia's greatest novelists are based on actual historical figures. Tolstoy appears to have first heard of the eponymous hero, Hadji Murat, in 1851, when, as a young army officer of twenty-three, he was serving in the Caucasus. This was the time when Hadji Murat's fame as one of Russia's most feared adversaries in the struggle for domination of that mountainous region on the Romanov empire's southern border was at its height. Tolstoy does not seem ever to have met the man, however, and his comment about him in a letter of December 1851 to his brother Sergei, where he refers to his defection to the Russians as 'a base action', does not immediately suggest him as a potential future fictional hero.

Yet Tolstoy evidently did not forget about Hadji Murat. For it was almost half a century later that, while walking near the country estate of that same brother Sergei, he came upon the thistle described in the prologue to the work in this volume and wrote the next day in his diary: 'It reminded me of Hadji Murat. I'd like to get it written.' Suddenly, in his late sixties, the spiritually troubled and often physically ailing grand old man of Russian letters was filled with a renewed sense of vigour as he returned to a theme that had recurred with some frequency in the works of his younger years. 'At difficult moments,' he wrote, 'everyone must battle, struggle, not give in.' And for the next eight years Tolstoy did indeed struggle with the epic theme of a man caught in a very different battle of his own: the clash between two peoples, the Caucasian tribesmen and the Russians; two faiths, Islam and Orthodox Christianity; and two rulers, the imam Shamil and the Emperor Nicholas I. Hadji Murat served a writer who was haunted, particularly in his later years, by the spectre of his own inevitable death as an emblem of the defiant individual refusing to submit meekly to powers beyond his control.

The hold that the theme of Hadji Murat exercised over Tolstoy between 1896 and 1904 is particularly remarkable in view of the author's at best ambivalent, and generally negative, attitude towards the genre of fiction in the closing decades of his life. He objected to the invention required in the composition of the novel, and considered it entirely inappropriate for a man of his age and standing. Thus he wrote to his wife late in 1897 that he was ashamed to be working on *Hadji Murat* – yet he had to confess that he could not leave it alone. Doubtless the historical basis of the story and the immense amount of research that he carried out to achieve as historically authentic a canvas as possible made *Hadji Murat* a less reprehensible sort of work in his eyes than the likes of *Anna Karenina*. In addition, the early stages of the composition of *Hadji Murat* coincided with Tolstoy's work on the treatise *What Is Art?*, and to some extent he seemed here to be producing a work of fiction that could satisfy the aesthetic demands he advocated of general accessibility and significance of content. Furthermore, his contention that 'the reason for the appearance of genuine art is the inner demand to express accumulated feeling' clearly boded well for the realisation of a theme that had been with him, albeit subconsciously, for almost all his adult life.

Certainly Tolstoy's inner demand to express the theme of struggle as illustrated by the fate of Hadji Murat must have been a very powerful one, for its execution was a long and painstaking process. And whereas the spiritual turmoil and ill health he suffered while engaged in the process must have reinforced his belief in the importance of his subject-matter, still they did not render the labour it demanded any easier. No fewer than ten distinct drafts, which in some cases differed drastically from the ones that preceded and followed, have been identified in the course of Tolstoy's work on what would eventually become the text presented here – and that figure does not take into account minor revisions and other less drastic editing processes. The first short draft entitled *The Thistle* dates from August 1896, but it was only with the fourth draft of November 1897 that the title *Hadji Murat* emerged. Later there was a break of three years between the sixth draft (March 1898) and the seventh (March 1901), in part a consequence of Tolstoy's work on the major novel *Resurrection*, but probably also an indication of the difficulty he was experiencing in resolving the basic question of how best to deal with his theme and its associated material. Hence, for instance, draft six was entitled *Holy War* and had the central theme of the betrayal of faith as the root cause of the hero's suffering, while draft eight was subtitled *The Memoirs of an Old Soldier* and had the narrative conducted by a young Russian officer. In the end, however, the years of reading, research, writing and rewriting bore fruit in the late summer of 1902, when in a period of seven weeks filled with creative energy Tolstoy produced in its essential structure, themes and language the work that we have today.

Perhaps one of the keys to this fulfilment of Tolstoy's oft-expressed determination to complete *Hadji Murat* lies in the circumstances of this period of his life. Just prior to his burst of concentrated work on *Hadji Murat*, Tolstoy had written the article 'To the Working People', in which he called upon them to engage in struggle to achieve their needs, in much the same way as he had himself been obliged to struggle to fight off serious illness throughout the previous year. He may have referred to *Hadji Murat* in a letter to his brother as 'indulgence and foolishness', but it was clearly a work that explored a theme then close to his heart. Indeed, if it seems odd that a man who preached non-violence should have been so committed to the completion of his portrayal of a life filled with bloodshed, then surely the answer to this riddle lies in Tolstoy's conviction that struggle was essential, be it with despotism, sexual appetite or the seeming absurdity of life. It is significant that the opening description of the encounter with the thistle remained virtually unaltered throughout all the years of drafting and redrafting, such was its value as the expression of the author's attitude to his material, of its central idea and poetic essence.

Despite his commitment to the completion of *Hadji Murat*, Tolstoy was under no illusions regarding the prospects for publication. He told his English biographer and translator Aylmer Maude as early as 1902 that his then uncompleted fictional works would remain unpublished during his lifetime as too much labour would be required of him to prepare them for final presentation to the public. His depiction of Prince Vorontsov, which became increasingly unsym-pathetic, and particularly of Nicholas I, after his inclusion in the fabric of the text during the intensive period of work in 1902, made publication of *Hadji Murat* under the conditions of Russian censor-ship quite unthinkable. In November 1902 Tolstoy wrote to his daughter that he had specifically decided not to print the work during his lifetime, but he nonetheless continued to collect new material, particularly on Nicholas I, make corrections and carry out revisions until the end of 1904.

However, *Hadji Murat* never did undergo comprehensive, systematic revision such as would have doubtless been carried out prior to publication. As a result, minor inconsistencies are to be found in the text, such as the length of time Hadji Murat spends in Major Petrov's fort, four days in Chapter 18 becoming a week in Chapter 20. Moreover there are some rough stylistic edges, the excessive repetition of the hero's name, for example, which should anyway come as no surprise since Tolstoy was not renowned as the most polished of the great Russian classics. But what Tolstoy did achieve in the process he described, using the term from painting, as 'touching up', was a text that is remarkably spare and taut and wonderfully vivid. Thus, although the adoption of a dignified, epic tone was the result of a decision made early on in the work's composition, it was through repeated revision that Hadji Murat's speech was made increasingly concise, while remaining colourful, and details of his biography came to emerge naturally rather than in exposition by the narrator. The opening *in medias res* is typical of the work's concentration on development through the depiction of action, being immediately exciting and plunging the reader into a situation that is mysterious and chaotic. The text is crammed with verbs, gerunds and participles which create a rare sense of dynamism and combine with brief, yet evocative descriptions of settings to produce an almost cinematic effect. There is very little to be found here of the inner thought processes of characters that play such an important part in the structure of Tolstoy's best-known novels: rather we have a simple story told in a straightforward way that is likely to have universal appeal in the manner of folktale or legend, with which it indeed has a great deal in common.

At one point in 1898 Tolstoy referred in his diary to the technique of the 'English "peep-show" ' – the kaleidoscope – as representing the most suitable method for depicting his central character as complex, changeable and multi-faceted; ultimately he did not carry this idea through, but arguably transferred the proposed technique for characterisation to the structuring of the work as a whole. Thus the reader is presented with a brilliant variety of different pictures that yet all have a common focus. Brief though it is, *Hadji Murat* is a work of massive scope, ranging from Caucasian forts and villages via the Russian countryside to the Winter Palace, and encompassing the lives of rulers and peasants, ordinary soldiers, both Russian and Chechen, and aristocratic officers. But above all it is a study of a figure, condemned by a young officer for what he discerned as 'a base action', who nevertheless became for a mature writer the very epitome of his conception of noble struggle.

– Hugh Aplin, 2003

Hadji Murat

I was returning home through the fields. It was the very height of summer. The meadows had been mown, and the rye was just about to be cut.

There is a delightful selection of flowers at that time of the year: red, white, and pink clover, fragrant and fluffy; impudent daisies; milky-white 'she-loves-me, she-loves-me-nots' with their bright yellow centres and their fusty, heady smell; yellow rape with its honeyed scent; lilac and white tulip-like campanula, tall and erect; creeping sweet peas; neat scabious, yellow, red, pink and lilac; plantain with a hint of pink down and a faint, pleasant smell; cornflowers, a bright deep blue in the sun and when young, but pale blue and flushed with red in the evening and when ageing; and the delicate almond-scented bindweed flowers that wither straight away.

I had gathered a large bunch of different flowers and was walking home when in a ditch I noticed in full bloom a wonderful crimson thistle of the sort that is called in Russia a 'Tatar', which people take pains to avoid when mowing, and which, when it is accidentally cut down, is thrown out of the hay by the mowers so that they do not prick their hands on it. I took it into my head to pick this thistle and put it in the middle of the bunch. I climbed down into the ditch and, driving off the fuzzy bumble-bee that had sunk itself into the heart of the flower where it had fallen into a sweet and languorous sleep, I set about picking the flower. But this was very difficult: not only did the stem prick me on all sides, even through the handkerchief in which I wrapped my hand, but it was so terribly strong that I struggled with it for some five minutes, tearing through the fibres one at a time. When I finally plucked the flower off, the stem was already quite ragged, and the flower no longer seemed so fresh and pretty either. Moreover, in its coarseness and clumsiness it did not go with the delicate flowers of the bunch. I felt regret at having needlessly ruined a flower which had been fine in its place, and I threw it away. 'Yet what energy and life-force,' I thought, recalling the effort with which I had picked the flower. 'How vigorously it defended, and how dearly it sold its life.'

The way home lay over a fallow, newly ploughed field of black earth. I went across it by a dusty black earth road. The ploughed field belonged to a landowner and was very large, so that on both sides of the road and on the slope ahead nothing could be seen except the black, evenly furrowed, still unbroken fallow. The ploughing had been done well, and nowhere across the field could there be seen a single plant or a single blade of grass – everything was black. 'What a destructive, cruel being man is, how many different living creatures and plants has he annihilated to sustain his own life,' I thought, involuntarily seeking out something living in the midst of this dead black field. In front of me, to the right of the road, some sort of little bush was visible. When I came closer I recognised in the little bush just such a 'Tatar' as that of which I had needlessly picked and discarded the flower.

The 'Tatar' bush consisted of three shoots. One had been torn off and the remnant of a stem stuck up like a severed arm. There was a flower on each of the other two. These flowers had once been red, but now they were black. One stem was broken, and half of it hung downwards with the dirty flower on the end; the other, although it too was daubed with black-earth mud, was still sticking upwards. It was evident that a wheel had driven over the entire bush, which had only afterwards picked itself up, and for that reason it was standing crookedly, but was standing nevertheless. It was as if it had had a piece of its body torn off, its innards turned inside out, its arm torn away, its eyes poked out. But it remains standing and does not surrender to man, who has destroyed all its brethren around it.

'What energy!' I thought. 'Man has conquered everything, destroyed millions of blades of grass, but this fellow refuses to surrender.'

And I was reminded of a story from long ago in the Caucasus, part of which I saw, part of which I heard from eyewitnesses, and part of which I imagined to myself. This story, in the way it has taken shape in my memory and imagination, is as follows.

1

It was at the end of 1851.

On a cold November evening Hadji Murat was riding into the hostile Chechen village of Mahket where pressed-dung fires were emitting their fragrant smoke.

The tense singing of the muezzin had only just died away, and in the

4

pure mountain air, impregnated with the smell of the smoke of pressed dung, beyond the lowing of the cows and the bleating of the sheep, scattered among the huts of the village which were stuck tight to one another like honeycomb, there could be heard distinctly from down below at the fountain the guttural sounds of arguing male voices and the voices of women and children.

This Hadji Murat was one of Shamil's[1] governors, renowned for his exploits, who never rode out other than with his pennant and accompanied by dozens of followers, all displaying their horsemanship around him. Now, wrapped up in a hood and felt cloak from beneath which there poked a rifle, he was riding with one follower, trying to be as inconspicuous as possible, gazing cautiously with his quick, black eyes into the faces of the inhabitants he encountered on his way.

Upon riding into the heart of the village, Hadji Murat did not continue along the street leading to the square, but turned left into a narrow lane. Riding up to the second hut in the lane, which was dug into the hillside, he stopped and looked around him. On the porch in front of the hut there was no one, but on the roof, behind the freshly oiled clay chimney there lay a man, covered in a sheepskin coat. Hadji Murat gave the man lying on the roof a light touch with the handle of his whip and clicked his tongue. From beneath the sheepskin there rose an old man in a nightcap and a shiny, torn quilted coat. The old man's eyes, lashless, were red and moist, and he blinked to get them unstuck. Hadji Murat pronounced the customary '*Seliam aleikum*' and revealed his face.

'*Aleikum seliam*,' said the old man with a toothless smile when he recognised Hadji Murat, and, getting to his bony feet, he began putting them into the wooden-heeled shoes that stood beside the chimney. Once shod, he unhurriedly put his arms into the sleeves of the wrinkled, uncovered sheepskin and climbed backwards down the ladder that leant against the roof. While both dressing and descending, the old man shook his head on his slender, wrinkled, tanned neck and muttered constantly with his toothless mouth. Stepping down onto the ground, he hospitably took hold of the rein of Hadji Murat's horse and his right stirrup. But, dismounting quickly, Hadji Murat's agile, powerful follower pushed the old man aside and took his place.

Hadji Murat dismounted and, limping slightly, went into the porch. There quickly emerged towards him from the door a boy of about fifteen, who stared in amazement at the new arrivals with shining eyes, black as ripe blackcurrants.

'Run to the mosque, call your father,' the old man ordered him and, forestalling Hadji Murat, opened the light door into the hut for him with a creak. As Hadji Murat was entering, from an inner door there emerged a slender, thin woman, no longer young, wearing a red quilted coat over a yellow shirt and blue trousers, and carrying some cushions.

'Your arrival is a sign of good fortune,' she said and, bending double, began laying out the cushions by the front wall for the guest to sit down.

'May your sons be alive,' replied Hadji Murat, who had taken off his cloak, rifle and sabre, and handed them to the old man.

The old man carefully hung the rifle and sabre on nails alongside the weapons of the hut's owner that were already hanging between two large basins, shining on the smoothly daubed, clean, whitewashed wall.

Adjusting the pistol behind his back, Hadji Murat went up to the cushions that the woman had laid out and, wrapping his Circassian coat about him, sat down on them. The old man squatted down opposite him on his bare heels and, closing his eyes, raised his hands with the palms uppermost. Hadji Murat did the same. Then, after saying a prayer, they both stroked their faces with their hands, bringing them together at the tips of their beards.

'*Ne khabar?*' enquired Hadji Murat of the old man, that is: 'what news?'

'*Khabar yok* – no news,' replied the old man, looking with his red, lifeless eyes not at Hadji Murat's face, but at his chest. 'I'm living at the bee-garden, I only came to visit my son today. He knows.'

Hadji Murat realised that the old man did not want to tell what he knew and what Hadji Murat needed to know, and with a slight nod of the head he asked no more.

'There's no good news,' began the old man. 'The only news is that all the hares are deliberating how they are to drive away the eagles, while the eagles keep on tearing apart first one, then another. Last week the

6

Russian dogs burned the Michik people's hay, rot their eyes,' wheezed the old man maliciously.

Hadji Murat's follower came in, stepped softly across the earthen floor with long strides of his powerful legs, and keeping on only his dagger and pistol, just like Hadji Murat he took off his cloak, rifle and sabre, and hung them up himself on the same nails on which Hadji Murat's weapons were hanging.

'Who is he?' the old man asked Hadji Murat, indicating the man who had come in.

'My follower. Eldar is his name,' said Hadji Murat.

'Very good,' said the old man, and indicated to Eldar a place on the strip of felt alongside Hadji Murat.

Eldar sat down, crossed his legs and stared silently with his beautiful sheep's eyes at the face of the now talkative old man. The old man told how their young men had last week caught two soldiers: one they had killed and the other they had sent to Shamil at Vedeno. Hadji Murat listened absent-mindedly, throwing glances at the door and listening intently to the noises outside. Steps were heard on the porch in front of the hut, the door creaked, and in came the hut's owner.

The owner of the hut, Sado, was a man of about forty with a little beard, a long nose and eyes that were just as black, although not so bright, as those of the fifteen-year-old boy, his son, who had run to fetch him, and, entering the hut together with his father, sat down by the door. Taking off his wooden shoes by the door, the host pushed his old, worn fur hat to the back of his head, long unshaven and covered in black hair, and immediately squatted down opposite Hadji Murat.

Just like the old man, he closed his eyes, raised his hands with the palms uppermost, said a prayer, wiped his face with his hands and only then began to speak. He said that there was an order from Shamil to detain Hadji Murat, dead or alive, that Shamil's messengers had left only the day before, that the people were afraid to disobey Shamil, and that for this reason it was necessary to be careful.

'In my house,' said Sado, 'nobody will do anything to my friend while I am alive. But what about in the open? We must think.'

Hadji Murat listened attentively and nodded in approval. When Sado had finished he said:

7

'Very good. Now I have to send a man to the Russians with a letter. My follower will go, only he needs a guide.'

'I'll send my brother, Bata,' said Sado. He turned to his son: 'Call Bata.'

As if on springs, the boy leapt to his lively feet and quickly left the hut, swinging his arms. About ten minutes later he returned with a darkly tanned, sinewy, short-legged Chechen in a disintegrating yellow Circassian coat with a ragged fringe on the sleeves and drooping black leggings. Hadji Murat greeted the newcomer and immediately, and with no wasted words either, said briefly:

'Can you take my follower to the Russians?'

'I can,' began Bata, quickly and cheerfully. 'I can do anything. There's not a single Chechen other than me will be able to get through. Anyone else will go and promise everything yet do nothing. But I can.'

'Good,' said Hadji Murat. 'You will have three for your trouble,' he said, sticking out three fingers.

Bata nodded to show that he had understood, but added that money did not matter to him, rather he was prepared to serve Hadji Murat for the honour. Everyone in the mountains knew Hadji Murat, how he had killed the Russian swine…

'Alright,' said Hadji Murat. 'A rope that is long is good, as is a speech that is short.'

'Well I'll keep quiet,' said Bata.

'Where the Argun bends, opposite the cliff, a clearing in the forest, there are two haystacks there. Do you know it?'

'I do.'

'My three horsemen are waiting for me there,' said Hadji Murat.

'Aha,' said Bata, nodding.

'Ask for Khan Magoma. Khan Magoma knows what to do and what to say. He is to be taken to the Russian leader, to Vorontsov, the Prince. Can you do it?'

'I'll take him.'

'Take him and bring him back. Can you do it?'

'I can.'

'You will take him and come back into the forest. And I shall be there.'

'I'll do it all,' said Bata, then stood up, put his hands to his chest and left.

'I need to send a man to Gekhi as well,' said Hadji Murat to his host when Bata had gone. 'This is what is needed in Gekhi,' he began, taking hold of one of the cartridge pouches on his coat, but he lowered his hand and fell silent when he saw two women had entered the hut.

One was Sado's wife, the same thin woman, no longer young, who had set out the cushions. The other was a very young girl in red trousers and a green quilted coat with a curtain of silver coins covering her entire breast. On the end of the coarse black plait, not long, but thick, that lay between the shoulders of her thin back, there hung a silver rouble; blackcurrant eyes, just as black as those of her father and brother, shone cheerfully in a young face that was trying to be severe. She did not look at the guests, but it was evident that she sensed their presence.

Sado's wife was carrying a low, round table on which were tea, stuffed dumplings, pancakes in butter, cheese, *churek* - flat bread – and honey. The girl was carrying a basin, a jug and a towel.

Sado and Hadji Murat both remained silent all the time that the women, moving quietly in their red soleless slippers, were setting out what they had brought before the guests. While Eldar, with his sheep's eyes fixed on his crossed legs, was motionless as a statue all the time that the women were in the hut. Only when the women had gone out and their soft footsteps had fallen completely quiet outside the door did Eldar heave a sigh of relief and Hadji Murat take hold of one of the cartridge pouches on his coat, take from it the bullet that filled it, and from beneath the bullet a rolled-up note.

'Give it to my son,' he said, indicating the note.

'Where does the reply go?'

'To you, and you will deliver it to me.'

'It will be done,' said Sado, and he transferred the note to a cartridge pouch on his coat. Then, taking the jug in his hands, he moved the basin towards Hadji Murat. Hadji Murat rolled up the sleeves of his quilted coat on his arms, muscular and white above the wrists, and put them under the stream of cold, clear water that Sado poured from the jug. Wiping his hands on the clean, rough towel, Hadji Murat moved closer to the food. Eldar did the same. While his guests were eating, Sado sat opposite them and thanked them several times for their visit. The boy sitting by the door did not take his shining black eyes off Hadji Murat and smiled, as if confirming with his smile the words of his father.

Despite the fact that Hadji Murat had eaten nothing for more than a day, he ate only a little bread and cheese and, getting some honey onto the small knife he had drawn from beneath his dagger, he spread it on some bread.

'Our honey's good. This year's honey above any other year's: there's a lot of it and it's good,' said the old man, evidently pleased that Hadji Murat was eating his honey.

'Thank you,' said Hadji Murat, and he sat back from the food.

Eldar wanted to eat some more, but he, just like his master, moved away from the table and handed Hadji Murat the basin and jug.

Sado knew that by entertaining Hadji Murat he was risking his life, because after the quarrel between Shamil and Hadji Murat all the inhabitants of Chechnya had been told, under threat of execution, not to receive Hadji Murat. He knew that the villagers might learn of Hadji Murat's presence in his home at any minute and might demand he be given up. But not only did this not worry Sado, it even pleased him. Sado considered it his duty to defend his guest – his friend – even if it cost him his life, and he was pleased with himself, proud of himself for behaving as he should.

'While you are in my home and my head is on my shoulders, nobody will do anything to you,' he repeated to Hadji Murat.

Hadji Murat looked attentively into his shining eyes and, realising that this was true, he said rather solemnly:

'May you be given joy and life.'

Sado put his hand to his chest in silence as a mark of gratitude for these kind words.

After closing the shutters of the hut and stoking up the logs in the fireplace, Sado left the guest-room in a particularly cheerful and excited state and entered the section of the hut where the whole of his family lived. The women were not yet asleep and were talking about the dangerous visitors spending the night in their guest-room.

2

That same night, fifteen kilometres from the village in which Hadji Murat was sleeping, a non-commissioned officer and three soldiers left the fortifications of the frontline fortress of Vozdvizhenskaya by the Chakhgirinsky gates. The soldiers wore sheepskin jackets, sheepskin hats and big boots that reached above the knee, as soldiers in the Caucasus did at that time, and had greatcoats rolled up over their shoulders. With rifles on their shoulders, the soldiers at first went along the road, then, having gone about five hundred paces, they turned off it and, with their boots rustling through the dry leaves, they went twenty paces or so to the right and stopped by a damaged plane tree, the black trunk of which could be seen even in the darkness. It was to this plane tree that listening posts were usually dispatched.

The bright stars that had seemed to be running along the treetops while the soldiers were going through the forest had now stopped, and shone brightly among the denuded branches of the trees.

'At least it's dry,' said the non-commissioned officer Panov, taking his long rifle with its bayonet down from his shoulder and, with a clatter, leaning it against the tree trunk. The three soldiers did the same.

'But I really have lost it,' grumbled Panov angrily, 'either I left it behind or it slipped out along the way.'

'What are you looking for?' asked one of the soldiers in a bright and cheerful voice.

'My pipe, the devil knows where it's got to!'

'Do you have the stem?' asked the cheerful voice.

'The stem – here it is.'

'What about putting it straight in the ground?'

'How's that then?'

'We'll sort it out quickly enough.'

Smoking was forbidden in a listening post, but this listening post was not really a listening post, more of a forward sentry post, sent out so that the mountaineers could not bring equipment up unnoticed, as they had done before, and fire at the fortifications, and Panov did not consider it necessary to deprive himself of a smoke, and so agreed to the cheerful soldier's proposal. The cheerful soldier took a knife out of his pocket and began digging in the ground. When he had dug out a small hole, he smoothed it around, brought the pipe stem up to it, then put some tobacco into the hole, pressed it down, and the pipe was ready. A sulphur match lit up, illuminating for a moment the prominent cheek-bones on the face of the soldier lying on his belly. A whistling began in the pipe stem, and Panov caught the pleasant scent of burning tobacco.

'Is it going?' he said, rising to his feet.

'Of course.'

'What a good fellow Avdeyev is! The lad's a real rascal. Well then?'

Avdeyev rolled away onto his side, allowing Panov to take his place, and let the smoke out of his mouth.

When they had had a good smoke, a conversation was struck up among the soldiers.

'They were saying the company commander has had his hand in the box again. Lost at cards, you see,' said one of the soldiers in a lazy voice.

'He'll pay it back,' said Panov.

'Of course, he's a good officer,' confirmed Avdeyev.

'A good one, a good one,' continued the one who had started the conversation gloomily, 'but my advice is, the company should have a word with him: if you've taken it, then say how much and when you'll pay it back.'

'As the company decides,' said Panov, tearing himself away from the pipe.

'Naturally, the community's the boss,' confirmed Avdeyev.

'You see, we'll need to buy oats and get boots repaired by the spring, we'll need the money, and as he's taken it…' insisted the discontented one.

'I'm saying, as the company wishes,' repeated Panov. 'It's not the first time: he'll go and pay it back.'

In the Caucasus in those days each company ran all its housekeeping itself through its own delegated men. It received money from the exchequer, six roubles and fifty kopeks per man, and supplied itself: it planted cabbages, mowed hay, maintained its own wagons, showed off the well-fed company horses. And the company's money was kept in a box, the keys to which were held by the company commander, and it was often the case that the company commander borrowed from the company box. That was what had happened now, and it was of this that the soldiers were talking. The gloomy soldier, Nikitin, wanted to demand a report from the company commander, while Panov and Avdeyev considered this unnecessary.

After Panov, Nikitin had a smoke too, then, spreading his greatcoat out beneath him, he sat down and leant against the tree. The soldiers fell quiet. All that could be heard was the wind stirring the treetops high above their heads. Suddenly, above this ceaseless gentle rustling, they heard the howling, squealing, crying and chuckling of jackals.

'Listen to the way they're roaring, damn them,' said Avdeyev.

'They're laughing at you because you've got a crooked snout,' came the reedy Ukrainian voice of the fourth soldier.

Again everything fell quiet, only the wind shifted the branches of the trees, now revealing, now concealing the stars.

'Well then, Antonych,' the cheerful Avdeyev suddenly asked Panov, 'are you ever miserable?'

'What do you mean by miserable?' replied Panov reluctantly.

'Well me, I'm just so miserable sometimes, so miserable that I don't think I even know for sure what I might do with myself.'

'Is that so?' said Panov.

'That time I spent all my money on drink, that was all out of being miserable. I just lost it, lost my mind. Why don't I get drunk, I thought.'

'But sometimes the wine just makes it worse.'

'That's happened to me. But what can you do?'

'What is it makes you feel like that?'

'Me? I get homesick.'

'What, well-off, were you?'

'We weren't exactly rich, but we managed. We had a good life.'

And Avdeyev began telling the story that he had already told to that same Panov many times.

'You know, I volunteered for the army in place of my brother,' said Avdeyev. 'He's got five kids! Whereas I'd only just got married. Mum asked me to. What's it to me, I thought! Perhaps my good deed'll be remembered. I went to see the master. We've got a good master, and he says: "Good lad! Off you go." So I went instead of my brother.'

'Well that's a good thing,' said Panov.

'But would you believe it, Antonych, now I'm miserable. And I'm miserable more than anything because I think: "Why did I go instead of my brother? He's bossing it now, and here you are suffering." And the more I think, the worse it is. I suppose it's my fault.'

Avdeyev paused.

'Shall we have another smoke then?'

'Alright, you set it going!'

But the soldiers did not get to have a smoke. Avdeyev had just stood up with a view to setting the pipe going again when, above the rustling of the wind, footsteps were heard from the road. Panov picked up his rifle and nudged Nikitin with his foot. Nikitin got to his feet and picked up his greatcoat. The third soldier, Bondarenko, stood up as well.

'What a dream I was having, lads…'

Avdeyev hissed at Bondarenko to be quiet and the soldiers froze, listening intently. The soft footsteps of men not wearing boots were approaching. The crackling of leaves and dry twigs could be heard more and more distinctly in the darkness. Then they heard voices talking in the peculiar guttural language spoken by the Chechens. The soldiers could now not only hear, but also see two shadows passing through the patch of light between trees. One shadow was a little shorter, the other a little taller. When the shadows came level with the soldiers, Panov, with his rifle resting on his arm, stepped out onto the road together with his two comrades.

'Who goes there?' he cried.

'Peaceful Chechen,' began the one who was shorter. It was Bata. 'No rifle. No sabre,' he said, pointing at himself. 'Need Per-rince.'

The one who was taller stood in silence alongside his comrade. He had no weapons either.

'A scout. To the regimental commander then,' said Panov, explaining to his comrades.

'Need Per-rince Vorontsov bad, need important matter,' said Bata.

'Alright, alright, we'll take you,' said Panov. He turned to Avdeyev: 'Well then, you and Bondarenko can take them, I suppose, and when you've handed them over to the duty officer, come back here again. Mind you take care,' said Panov, 'order them to walk in front of you. Because these shaven-heads, you know – they're full of tricks.'

'What's this then?' said Avdeyev, making a stabbing movement with his rifle and bayonet. 'One jab and I'll let the steam out.'

'And what use will he be if you stab him?' said Bondarenko. 'Come on, forward march!'

When the footsteps of the two soldiers and the scouts had fallen quiet, Panov and Nikitin returned to their place.

'The devil's got into them, wandering round at night!' said Nikitin.

'It must have been vital,' said Panov. 'It's turned fresh though,' he added, and, unrolling his greatcoat, he put it on and sat down against the tree.

Avdeyev and Bondarenko returned about two hours later.

'Well then, did you hand them over?' asked Panov.

'We did. They were still awake at the regimental commander's. They were taken straight to him. But what good lads those shaven-heads are, my old mate!' continued Avdeyev. 'Honest to God! I had such a good chat with them.'

'You're bound to have had a good chat,' said Nikitin, discontentedly.

'They're just like Russians really. One's married. *Marushka*, I says, *bar*? – *Bar*, he says. – *Baranchuk*, I says, *bar*? – *Bar*. – Many kids? – A couple, he says. – We had such a good chat. Good lads.'

'What do you mean, good,' said Nikitin, 'just you come across him one to one and he'll spill your guts out.'

'It should be getting light soon,' said Panov.

'Yes, the stars have started going out,' said Avdeyev, sitting himself down.

And the soldiers fell quiet once more.

3

In the windows of the barracks and the soldiers' houses it had already long been dark, but in one of the best houses in the fortress all the windows were still lit up. This house was occupied by the commander of the Kurinsky regiment, the son of the commander-in-chief, aide-de-camp Prince Semyon Mikhailovich Vorontsov. Vorontsov lived with his wife, Maria Vasilyevna, a renowned St Petersburg beauty, and lived in the small Caucasian fortress a life of such luxury as no one had ever lived here before. It seemed to Vorontsov and in particular to his wife that they led here not only a modest life, but one filled with privations; whereas this life amazed the local inhabitants by its unusual luxury.

Now, at midnight, in the large drawing-room with a carpet the size of the entire room, with the heavy *portières* lowered, the host and hostess were sitting playing cards with their guests at a card-table lit by four candles. One of the players was the host himself, the fair-haired colonel with a long face, wearing his aide-de-camp's monograms and aiguillettes, Vorontsov; his partner was the holder of a degree from the University of St Petersburg, a shaggy youth of morose appearance, the tutor recently summoned by Princess Vorontsova for her young son by her first husband. Playing against them were two officers: one was the broad-faced, ruddy company commander Poltoratsky who had been transferred from the Guards, and the other was the regimental adjutant, who sat very straight with a cold expression on his handsome face. Princess Maria Vasilyevna herself, a statuesque, big-eyed, black-browed beauty, sat alongside Poltoratsky, touching his legs with her crinoline and looking at his cards. Both in her words and in her looks, in her smile and in every movement of her body, and in the scent of her perfume, there was something that led Poltoratsky to forget everything except his consciousness of her proximity, and he made mistake after mistake, irritating his partner more and more.

'No, it's not possible! He's wasted an ace again!' the adjutant blurted out, turning quite red, when Poltoratsky discarded an ace.

As if he had just woken up, Poltoratsky gazed in bewilderment with his kind, widely set black eyes at the displeased adjutant.

'Do forgive him!' said Maria Vasilyevna with a smile. She turned to Poltoratsky: 'You see, I told you.'

'But you said nothing of the sort,' said Poltoratsky with a smile.

'Did I not?' she said, and smiled as well. And this smile in response agitated and delighted Poltoratsky so terribly that he flushed crimson and, seizing the cards, began shuffling them.

'It's not your turn to shuffle,' said the adjutant sternly, and with his white hand sporting a signet-ring he began to deal the cards in a manner that suggested he only wanted to be rid of them quickly.

The Prince's valet entered the drawing-room and announced that the duty officer was asking for the Prince.

'Excuse me, gentlemen,' said Vorontsov, speaking Russian with an English accent. 'You can take my seat, Marie.'

'Do you agree?' asked the Princess, rising quickly and easily to her considerable full height, with her silk rustling, and smiling the radiant smile of a happy woman.

'I always agree to everything,' said the adjutant, very pleased at the fact that against him now would be playing the Princess, who did not know how to play at all. And Poltoratsky merely spread his hands with a smile.

The rubber was drawing to a close when the Prince returned to the drawing-room. He arrived looking particularly cheerful and excited.

'Do you know what I'm going to suggest to you?'

'Well?'

'Let's have some champagne.'

'I'm always game for that,' said Poltoratsky.

'Well, that's very pleasant,' said the adjutant.

'Vasily! Serve it up!' said the Prince.

'Why were you called?' asked Maria Vasilyevna.

'It was the duty officer and another man.'

'Who was it? What was it?' asked Maria Vasilyevna hurriedly.

'I can't say,' said Vorontsov, shrugging his shoulders.

'You can't say,' repeated Maria Vasilyevna. 'We'll see about that.'

Champagne was brought. The guests drank a glass each and, after finishing the game and settling up, they began making their farewells.

'Is it your company assigned to the forest tomorrow?' the Prince asked Poltoratsky.

'Mine. What of it?'

'Then we shall see one another tomorrow,' said the Prince with a faint smile.

'Delighted,' said Poltoratsky, without understanding very well what Vorontsov was saying to him, and preoccupied only with how he was now going to clasp Maria Vasilyevna's large white hand.

Maria Vasilyevna, as always, not only clasped Poltoratsky's hand tightly, but also gave it a firm shake. And reminding him once again of his mistake when he started playing diamonds, she smiled at him, as it seemed to Poltoratsky, a smile that was delightful, tender and meaningful.

Poltoratsky walked home in that exultant mood that can only be understood by men who, like him, have grown and been raised in society, when, after months of isolated military life, they encounter once more a woman from their former circle. And such a woman, what is more, as Princess Vorontsova.

Going up to the house in which he lived with a comrade, he pushed the front door, but the door was locked. He knocked. No one unlocked the door. He became annoyed and began to drum on the locked door with his foot and sabre. Footsteps were heard on the other side of the door, and Vavilo, Poltoratsky's house-serf, threw back the catch.

'What gave you the idea of locking it?! Blockhead!'

'But how can you, Alexei Vladimir...'

'Drunk again! Now I'll show you how I can...' Poltoratsky meant to hit Vavilo, but changed his mind.

'Oh, to hell with you. Light a candle.'

'Shtraight 'way.'

Vavilo was indeed drunk, and he had been drinking because he had been at the quartermaster-sergeant's name-day party. On returning home, he fell into thought about his life in comparison with the life of Ivan Makeyich, the quartermaster-sergeant. Ivan Makeyich had an income, was married, and hoped in a year's time to retire for good. Whereas Vavilo had been taken up, taken into service with his masters that is, as a boy, and now he was already past forty, yet he had not married and he lived his life on campaign with his messy master. He was a good master, did not beat him much, but what sort of a life was this! 'He promised to give me my freedom when he leaves the Caucasus. But where am I to go with my freedom? It's a dog's life!' thought Vavilo. And he wanted to sleep so badly that, afraid somebody might come in and steal something, he put the catch down and fell asleep.

Poltoratsky went into the room where he slept together with his comrade, Tikhonov.

'Well, did you lose?' said Tikhonov, waking up.

'Not at all. I won seventeen roubles, and we drank a bottle of Clicquot.'

'And you gazed at Maria Vasilyevna?'

'And I gazed at Maria Vasilyevna,' repeated Poltoratsky.

'Time to be getting up soon,' said Tikhonov, 'and at six we should already be moving out.'

'Vavilo!' shouted Poltoratsky. 'Mind you wake me up properly tomorrow at five.'

'How am I to wake you up when you hit me?'

'I'm telling you to wake me up. D'you hear?'

'As you say.'

Vavilo left, carrying boots and clothing.

And Poltoratsky got into bed and, smiling, lit up a cigarette and put out the candle. Before him in the darkness he saw the smiling face of Maria Vasilyevna.

They did not go to sleep straight away at the Vorontsovs' either. When their guests had left, Maria Vasilyevna went up to her husband and, stopping in front of him, said sternly:

'*Eh bien, vous allez me dire ce que c'est?*'

'*Mais, ma chère…*'

'*Pas de "ma chère"! C'est un émissaire, n'est-ce pas?*'

'*Quand même, je ne puis pas vous le dire.*'

'*Vous ne pouvez pas? Alors c'est moi qui vais vous le dire.*'

'*Vous?*'[2]

'Hadji Murat? Yes?' said the Princess, who had been hearing for several days now about negotiations with Hadji Murat and assumed that Hadji Murat himself had been with her husband.

Vorontsov could not deny it, but disenchanted his wife with the fact that it had not been Hadji Murat himself, but only a scout, who had announced that Hadji Murat would ride out to see him tomorrow at the place assigned for felling trees.

Amidst the monotony of life in the fortress the young Vorontsovs – both husband and wife – were very pleased about this event. Having talked of how pleasant this news would be for his father, husband and wife went to bed some time after two o'clock.

4

Following the three sleepless nights that he had spent fleeing from the men sent out against him by Shamil, Hadji Murat fell asleep immediately, the moment that Sado left the hut, wishing him good-night. He slept without getting undressed, resting on his arm, with his elbow sunk into the red down-filled cushions that his host had set out for him. Not far away from him, by the wall, slept Eldar. Eldar lay on his back with his strong young limbs spread wide, so that his deep chest with the black cartridge pouches on his white Circassian coat was higher than his newly shaven, blue head, which, cast back, had slipped off his pillow. It was as if his upper lip, protruding like a child's and barely covered by a light down, were sipping something, as it tightened, and then relaxed. He slept in his clothes, just like Hadji Murat, with his pistol in his belt and his dagger. In the hut's fireplace the wood was burning down, and in the stove the night-light was just visible.

In the middle of the night the door into the guest-room creaked, and Hadji Murat immediately rose and took hold of his pistol. Into the room, stepping softly across the earthen floor, came Sado.

'What do you want?' asked Hadji Murat brightly, as if he had never been asleep.

'We need to think,' said Sado, squatting down in front of Hadji Murat. 'A woman saw you arrive from her roof,' he said, 'and she told her husband, and now the whole village knows. A neighbour came in quickly to see my wife just now, and said that the old men had gathered by the mosque and wanted to stop you.'

'I must go,' said Hadji Murat.

'The horses are ready,' said Sado, and quickly went out of the hut.

'Eldar,' whispered Hadji Murat, and Eldar, hearing his name and, most importantly, the voice of his master, leapt up on his powerful legs, adjusting his sheepskin hat. Hadji Murat put on his weapons and cloak. Eldar did the same. And both went out of the hut onto the porch in silence. The black-eyed boy brought forward the horses. At the clatter of hooves on the beaten roadway of the street somebody's head was poked out from the door of a neighbouring hut, and, his wooden shoes clattering, a man ran past up the hill towards the mosque.

There was no moon, but the stars were shining brightly in the black sky, and in the darkness the outlines of the roofs of the huts were visible, as was, more than any, the building of the mosque with its minaret in the upper part of the village. From the mosque there carried the rumble of voices.

Hadji Murat quickly seized his rifle, set his foot in the narrow stirrup, and, noiselessly, with an imperceptible movement of his body, he sat himself on the high cushion of the saddle.

'May God repay you!' he said, turning to his host while seeking the other stirrup with a customary movement of his right foot, and he touched the boy who was holding the horse ever so lightly with his whip as a sign that he should step aside. The boy stepped aside, and the horse, as though it knew what it was to do itself, moved off at a lively pace out of the lane onto the main road. Eldar rode behind; Sado, in his fur coat and swinging his arms rapidly, was almost running after them, slipping first to one, then to the other side of the narrow street. At the exit there appeared across the road one moving shadow, then another.

'Halt! Who's that? Stop!' cried a voice, and several men blocked the road.

Instead of stopping, Hadji Murat pulled his pistol out from his belt and, increasing his pace, directed the horse straight at the men blocking the road. The men standing in the road parted, and Hadji Murat, without looking round, set off down the road at a good canter. Eldar rode after him at a fast trot. Behind them the cracks of two shots rang out, and two bullets whistled past, hitting neither him, nor Eldar. Hadji Murat continued to ride at the same speed. When he was some three hundred paces away, he halted his horse, which was panting slightly, and began listening carefully. Ahead, down below, was the noise of fast running water. Behind, cockerels could be heard calling to one another in the village. Audible above these sounds behind Hadji Murat were the approaching clatter of horses' hooves and voices. Hadji Murat set his horse moving and rode off at the same even pace.

Those riding behind were galloping and soon overtook Hadji Murat. There were about twenty horsemen. They were the inhabitants of the village who had decided to detain Hadji Murat or at least, to clear themselves with Shamil, to pretend that they meant to detain him.

When they had come so close that they were visible in the darkness, Hadji Murat stopped, dropped his reins, and, undoing his rifle-holster with a customary movement of the left hand, he took the rifle out with his right hand. Eldar did the same.

'What do you want?' cried Hadji Murat. 'Do you want to take me? Well take me then!' And he raised his rifle. The inhabitants of the village stopped.

Holding his rifle in his hand, Hadji Murat began the descent into a depression. The men on horseback rode after him without gaining ground. When Hadji Murat had crossed to the other side of the depression, the horsemen following him called out to him to hear out what they wanted to say. In reply to this Hadji Murat fired his rifle and set his horse off at a gallop. When he stopped it, the pursuit behind him could no longer be heard; the cockerels could not be heard either, but more clearly audible now were the babbling of water in the forest and the occasional cry of an eagle owl. The black wall of the forest was very close. This was that same forest in which his followers were waiting for him. Riding up to the forest, Hadji Murat stopped and, drawing a considerable quantity of air into his lungs, he let out a whistle and then fell silent, listening intently. After a minute the same whistling rang out from the forest. Hadji Murat turned off the road and set off into the forest. When he had ridden a hundred paces or so, Hadji Murat caught sight between the tree trunks of a camp-fire, the shadows of men sitting by the fire, and a horse, half lit up by the fire, hobbled and saddled.

One of the men sitting by the camp-fire got up quickly, came over to Hadji Murat, and took hold of his rein and stirrup. This was Khanefi, an Avar, Hadji Murat's sworn brother who looked after his belongings.

'Put the fire out,' said Hadji Murat, dismounting. The men began breaking up the camp-fire and trampling on the burning branches.

'Has Bata been here?' asked Hadji Murat, going up to a felt cloak laid out on the ground.

'He has, he left a long time ago with Khan Magoma.'

'What road did they take?'

'This one,' replied Khanefi, indicating the opposite direction to that from which Hadji Murat had arrived.

'Good,' said Hadji Murat, and, taking off his rifle, he began loading it. 'We need to take care; they came after me,' he said, addressing the man putting out the fire.

He was a Chechen, Gamzalo. Gamzalo went over to the cloak, picked up the rifle that was lying on it in its holster, and walked silently to the edge of the clearing, to the spot from which Hadji Murat had ridden up. Eldar got down from his horse, took Hadji Murat's horse and, pulling both of their heads up high, he tied them to trees; then, just like Gamzalo, he took up a position on the other side of the clearing with his rifle behind his shoulders. The camp-fire was extinguished, and the forest no longer seemed so black as before, and in the sky, albeit weakly, the stars were shining.

Looking at the stars, at the Pleiades which were already halfway up the sky, Hadji Murat calculated that it was well past midnight and that it was already high time for the night's prayers. He asked Khanefi for the jug that was always carried in his baggage and, putting on his cloak, he walked off towards the water.

After taking off his shoes and performing his ablutions, Hadji Murat stood barefooted on his cloak, then squatted down and, having first put his fingers in his ears and closed his eyes, turning to the east, he said his usual prayers.

When he had finished praying, he returned to the spot where his saddle bags were, sat down on his cloak, leant his arms on his knees and, lowering his head, fell into thought.

Hadji Murat had always believed in his own good fortune. Whenever he undertook anything, he was firmly convinced of its success in advance – and he was successful in everything. So had it been, with rare exceptions, during the whole of his stormy military life. So, he hoped, would it be now too. He pictured to himself how, with the troops that Vorontsov would give him, he would march on Shamil and take him prisoner, take revenge on him, and how the Russian Tsar would reward him, and he would rule once more not only Avaria, but the whole of Chechnya too, which would submit to him. With these thoughts he did not notice he had fallen asleep.

He dreamed of falling upon Shamil with his warriors, with singing and with the cry 'here comes Hadji Murat', of capturing him and his wives and hearing his wives wail and sob. He woke up. The song

'*Lya illyakha*' and the cries of 'here comes Hadji Murat' and the wailing of Shamil's wives – these were the howling, the crying, and the chuckling of the jackals that had woken him. Hadji Murat raised his head, glanced at the sky that was already lightening in the east between the tree trunks, and asked the follower sitting a little distance away from him about Khan Magoma. Learning that Khan Magoma had not yet returned, Hadji Murat lowered his head and immediately dozed off once more.

He was woken up by the cheerful voice of Khan Magoma, returning with Bata from his embassy. Khan Magoma immediately sat down next to Hadji Murat and began recounting how they had been met by soldiers and taken to the Prince himself, how he had spoken with the Prince himself, how the Prince had been pleased and promised to meet them in the morning in the place where the Russians would be cutting wood, beyond the Michik River, at the Shalinskaya clearing. Bata interrupted his partner's speech, putting in his own details.

Hadji Murat asked detailed questions about precisely what words Vorontsov had used in reply to Hadji Murat's proposal to go over to the Russians. Both Khan Magoma and Bata said in one voice that the Prince had promised to receive Hadji Murat as a guest and to do everything to make him feel comfortable. Hadji Murat questioned them further about the way, and when Khan Magoma assured him that he knew the way well and would lead him straight there, Hadji Murat got out some money and handed Bata the promised three roubles; and he ordered his own men to get out from the saddle-bags his gold inlaid weapons and his sheepskin hat and turban, and told the followers to clean themselves up so as to look good when appearing before the Russians. By the time they had cleaned their weapons, saddles, harness and horses, the stars had faded altogether; it had become quite light, and the pre-dawn breeze had risen.

5

Early in the morning, while it was still dark, two companies with axes under the command of Poltoratsky went more than ten kilometres out of the Chakhgirinsky gates and, scattering out a line of marksmen, as soon as it began to get light they set about felling trees. By eight o'clock

24

the mist, merging with the fragrant smoke of the dry branches hissing and cracking on the camp-fires, began to lift, and the woodcutters, who had previously not been able to see, but only to hear one another at more than five paces, began to see both the camp-fires and the road through the forest, covered with heaps of trees; the sun would now appear as a bright spot in the mist, now disappear again. Sitting on drums in a clearing a short distance from the road were Poltoratsky and his subaltern, Tikhonov, two officers of the Third Company and a former horse-guardsman who had been transferred because of a duel, a friend of Poltoratsky's from the Corps des Pages, Baron Freze. Around the drums lay the scattered wrappings from food, cigarette-ends and empty bottles. The officers had drunk some vodka, had a bite to eat, and were now drinking porter. A drummer was opening the eighth bottle. Despite the fact that he had not had enough sleep, Poltoratsky was in that mood of enhanced spiritual powers and genial, carefree gaiety in which he always found himself when among his soldiers and comrades in a place where there might be danger.

An animated conversation was underway among the officers about the latest news, the death of General Sleptsov. Nobody saw in this death that most important moment in life – its conclusion and return to the source from which it had come; rather they saw only the mettle of a dashing officer who had hurled himself at mountaineers with his sabre, hacking at them in desperation.

Although they all, especially the officers who had seen action, knew and were in a position to know that neither in the war in the Caucasus at that time, nor indeed anywhere at any time, was there any of that hand-to-hand hacking with sabres which is always imagined and described (and even if there is such hand-to-hand fighting with sabres and bayonets, then it is always and only those who are fleeing that are hacked and stabbed), this fiction of hand-to-hand fighting was acknowledged by the officers and lent them that calm pride and cheerfulness with which they sat on the drums, some in dashing, others, by contrast, in the most modest poses, smoked, drank and joked, not worrying about the death which might at any minute strike down each of them, just as it had Sleptsov. And indeed, as if in confirmation of their expectation, in the middle of their conversation, there rang out to the left of the road the invigorating, attractive sound of a rifle shot's sharp crack, and the bullet, whistling cheerfully, flew by somewhere in the misty air and cracked into a tree. Several loud and heavy shots from soldiers' rifles replied to the enemy shot.

'Aha!' cried Poltoratsky, in a cheerful voice, 'that's in the line, you know! Well, Kostya, my friend,' he turned to Freze, 'it's your good fortune. Go and join the company. We'll organise such an engagement shortly, it'll be a delight! And we'll put on a show.'

The demoted baron leapt to his feet, and set off at a fast pace to the area of smoke where his company was. Poltoratsky had his dark-bay Kabardian horse led forward, he mounted it and, forming the company up, he led it towards the line in the direction of the shots. The line stood on the edge of the forest in front of a downward sloping, bare gully. The wind was blowing towards the forest, and not only the downslope of the gully, but also its other side were both clearly visible.

When Poltoratsky rode up to the line, the sun peeped out from behind the mist, and on the opposite side of the gully, by another small wood that began there, more than two hundred metres away, several horsemen could be seen. These Chechens were the ones who had pursued Hadji Murat and wanted to see his meeting with the Russians. One of them had shot at the line. Several soldiers in the line had replied to him. The Chechens had moved away again and the shooting had ceased. But when Poltoratsky came up with his company, he gave the order to fire, and no sooner had the command been given, than along the whole length of the line there could be heard the incessant, cheerful, invigorating crackling of rifles, accompanied by attractively diffusing puffs of smoke. The soldiers, pleased with the diversion, hurried their loading and fired round after round. The Chechens evidently sensed the enthusiasm and, galloping forward, one after another they fired several shots at the soldiers. One of their shots wounded a soldier. This soldier was that same Avdeyev who had been in the listening post. When his comrades approached him he was lying with his back uppermost, holding the wound in his stomach with both hands and evenly rocking a little from side to side.

'I'd just started loading my rifle and I heard a clunk,' the soldier who had been paired with him was saying. 'I looked and he'd dropped his rifle.'

Avdeyev was from Poltoratsky's company. Seeing the knot of soldiers that had gathered, Poltoratsky rode up to them.

'What, are you hit, my friend?' he said. 'Where?'

Avdeyev did not reply.

'I'd just started loading, Your Honour,' began the soldier who had been paired with Avdeyev, 'and I heard a clunk, and I looked, and he'd dropped his rifle.'

'Tut, tut,' Poltoratsky clicked his tongue. 'Well, are you in pain, Avdeyev?'

'Not in pain, but I can't walk. Some wine'd help, Your Honour.'

Vodka – that is the spirit that soldiers drank in the Caucasus – was found, and Panov, frowning severely, offered Avdeyev the spirit in a bottle cap. Avdeyev started to drink, but immediately pushed the cap away with his hand.

'Can't take it,' he said. 'Drink yourself.'

Panov drank the rest of the spirit. Again Avdeyev tried to get up and again he sat down. A greatcoat was spread out and Avdeyev was put on it.

'Your Honour, the colonel's coming,' said the sergeant-major to Poltoratsky.

'Alright, you deal with things,' said Poltoratsky, and with a wave of his whip he set off at a fast trot to meet Vorontsov.

Vorontsov was riding his English thoroughbred chestnut stallion and was accompanied by the regimental adjutant, a Cossack and a Chechen interpreter.

'What's going on here?' he asked Poltoratsky.

'A group came out and attacked the line,' Poltoratsky answered him.

'Aha, and it was all your doing.'

'Not mine, Prince,' said Poltoratsky with a smile, 'they wanted it themselves.'

'I hear a soldier's been wounded?'

'Yes, it's a great pity. He's a good soldier.'

'Is it serious?'

'I think so – the stomach.'

'And do you know where I'm going?' asked Vorontsov.

'No, I don't.'

'Surely you can guess?'

'No.'

'Hadji Murat has come over and will shortly be meeting us.'

'It's not possible!'

'There was a scout from him yesterday,' said Vorontsov, having difficulty containing a smile of joy. 'He should be waiting for me now at the Shalinskaya clearing; so scatter your marksmen out as far as the clearing and then come and join me.'

'Yes, sir!' said Poltoratsky, bringing his hand up to his sheepskin hat, and rode off to his company. He himself led the line away to the right and ordered the sergeant-major to do so on the left. Meanwhile four soldiers carried the wounded man off to the fortress.

Poltoratsky was already returning to Vorontsov when he saw some horsemen overtaking him from behind. Poltoratsky stopped to wait for them.

Ahead of them all on a white-maned horse, wearing a white Circassian coat, a turban on his sheepskin hat and weapons decorated with gold, rode a man of impressive appearance. This man was Hadji Murat. He rode up to Poltoratsky and said something to him in Tatar. Poltoratsky raised his eyebrows, spread his hands to signify that he did not understand, and smiled. Hadji Murat replied to his smile with a smile, and this smile amazed Poltoratsky by its childlike amiability. Poltoratsky had not at all expected to see the terrifying mountaineer behaving like this. He had expected a gloomy, dry, alien man, yet before him was the simplest of men, smiling such a kind smile that he seemed not a stranger, but a friend of long standing. There was only one extraordinary thing about him: that was his wide-set eyes, which looked attentively, shrewdly and calmly into the eyes of other men.

Hadji Murat's suite consisted of four men. The suite included the same Khan Magoma who that night had gone to see Vorontsov. He was a ruddy, round-faced man with bright, black, lidless eyes, who glowed with an expression of *joie de vivre*. There was also a thickset, hairy man with eyebrows that joined together. This was Khanefi the Tavlin, who was in charge of all Hadji Murat's belongings. With him he led a spare horse with tightly packed saddle-bags. But two men in the suite stood out in particular: one was young, slender as a woman in the waist and broad in the shoulder, with a light-brown beard only just coming through, a handsome man with sheep's eyes – this was Eldar; and the other, blind in one eye, without eyebrows or eyelashes, with a trimmed red beard and a scar across his face and nose – the Chechen Gamzalo.

Poltoratsky pointed out to Hadji Murat the figure of Vorontsov who had appeared further down the road. Hadji Murat set off in his direction and, when he had come up alongside him, he put his right hand to his chest, said something in Tatar and stopped. The Chechen interpreter translated:

'I give myself up, he says, to the will of the Russian Tsar, I want, he says, to serve him. Have wanted to for a long time, he says. Shamil would not let him go.'

After hearing out the interpreter, Vorontsov extended his suede-gloved hand to Hadji Murat. Hadji Murat looked at this hand, delayed for a second, but then squeezed it firmly and said something more, gazing now at the interpreter, now at Vorontsov.

'He says he did not want to surrender to anyone but you alone, because you are the son of the chief. He respected you greatly.'

Vorontsov nodded to signify that he was grateful. Hadji Murat said something else, pointing to his suite.

'He says that these men, his followers, will serve the Russians just like him.'

Vorontsov looked around at them and nodded to them too.

Cheerful Khan Magoma with the black, lidless eyes, nodding his head as well, must have said something funny to Vorontsov, because the hairy Avar bared his brilliant white teeth in a smile. But red-haired Gamzalo only flashed his one red eye at Vorontsov for a moment, then fixed his stare once more on the ears of his horse.

As Vorontsov and Hadji Murat, accompanied by his suite, were riding back to the fortress, the soldiers who had been withdrawn from the line and had gathered together in a knot were making their comments:

'How many souls has he sent to perdition, the devil, and now they'll be trying to keep him sweet, I shouldn't wonder,' said one.

'What do you expect? He was Sam Eel's number one commander. Now, I suppose…'

'But you've got to admit it, the young horseman's a big lad.'

'And what about the ginger one – looks at you sidelong like a wild animal.'

'Oh, a real dog, I expect.'

They had all noticed the ginger one in particular.

Where the felling was taking place, the soldiers who were closest to the road ran out to take a look. Their officer shouted at them, but Vorontsov stopped him.

'Let them look at their old acquaintance. Do you know who this is?' asked Vorontsov of the soldier standing nearest, pronouncing the words slowly with his English accent.

'No, Your Highness.'

'Hadji Murat – have you heard of him?'

'Of course I have, Your Highness, we've attacked him lots of times.'

'Well, and we've had to take it from him.'

'Yes, Your Highness,' replied the soldier, pleased at having managed to have a talk with his leader.

Hadji Murat understood that they were talking about him, and a cheerful smile shone in his eyes. Vorontsov returned to the fortress in the most cheerful frame of mind.

6

Vorontsov was very pleased that it was he, none other than he, that had succeeded in luring out and receiving Russia's second most important and powerful enemy after Shamil. There was one unpleasant thing: the commander of the troops in Vozdvizhenskaya was General Meller-Zakomelsky, and, in reality, the whole matter should have been conducted through him. But Vorontsov had done everything himself without informing him, so there might be some trouble. And this thought poisoned Vorontsov's pleasure somewhat.

On riding up to his house, Vorontsov entrusted Hadji Murat's followers to the regimental adjutant, and himself led Hadji Murat into his home.

Princess Maria Vasilyevna greeted Hadji Murat in the dining-room wearing her finery and smiling, together with her son, a handsome, curly-haired boy of six, and Hadji Murat, putting his hands to his chest, said rather solemnly through the interpreter who had come in with him, that he considered himself the Prince's friend since he had received him in his house, and that the entire family of a friend was just as sacred for a friend as he himself. Maria Vasilyevna liked both Hadji Murat's appearance and manners. And the fact that he blushed and turned quite red when she gave him her large white hand disposed her still further in his favour. She asked him to sit down and, enquiring whether he drank coffee, she ordered it to be served. However, Hadji Murat refused the coffee when it was served to him. He understood Russian a little but could not speak it, and when he did not understand he smiled, and Maria Vasilyevna liked his smile, just as Poltoratsky had. And Maria Vasilyevna's curly-haired, sharp-eyed little son, called Crumpet by his mother, stood alongside his mother and did not take his eyes off Hadji Murat, whom he had heard to be an extraordinary warrior.

Leaving Hadji Murat with his wife, Vorontsov went to his office to make arrangements for informing his superiors about Hadji Murat's surrender. After writing a report to General Kozlovsky, the commander of the left flank in Grozny, and a letter to his father, Vorontsov hurried home, fearing his wife's displeasure at having thrust upon her a terrifying stranger, who needed to be treated in such a way so as not to offend, yet without being too nice. But his fear was misplaced. Hadji Murat was sitting in an armchair, holding Crumpet, Vorontsov's stepson, on his knee, and, with his head inclined, was listening attentively to what the interpreter was saying to him in conveying the words of the laughing Maria Vasilyevna. Maria Vasilyevna was telling him that if he gave to every friend the thing of his that the friend praised, then he would soon have to go around like Adam...

At the entrance of the Prince, Hadji Murat removed Crumpet, who was surprised and offended by this, from his knee and stood up, immediately exchanging his playful expression for a stern and serious one. He sat down only when Vorontsov did. Continuing their conversation, he replied to Maria Vasilyevna's words that such was their law, that all that a friend liked must be given to the friend.

'Your son is my friend,' he said in Russian, stroking Crumpet's curly hair when the boy climbed back onto his knee.

'Your brigand is delightful,' said Maria Vasilyevna to her husband in French. 'Crumpet started admiring his dagger, and he presented it to him.'

Crumpet showed the present to his stepfather.

'*C'est un objet de prix,*'[3] said Maria Vasilyevna.

'*Il faudra trouver l'occasion de lui faire cadeau,*'[4] said Vorontsov.

Hadji Murat sat with his eyes cast down and, stroking the boy's curly head, kept saying in Tatar:

'Horseman, horseman.'

'A beautiful dagger, beautiful,' said Vorontsov, half drawing the sharpened damask steel blade with a groove down the centre. 'Thank you.'

'Ask him how I can be of service to him,' said Vorontsov to the interpreter.

The interpreter conveyed this, and Hadji Murat immediately replied that he needed nothing, but that he would now like to be taken to a place where he could pray. Vorontsov called his valet and ordered him to carry out Hadji Murat's wish.

As soon as Hadji Murat was left alone in the room made available to him, his face altered: the expression of pleasure and alternating tenderness and solemnity vanished, and there appeared an expression of anxiety.

The reception given him by Vorontsov was much better than he had expected. But the better the reception was, the less Hadji Murat trusted Vorontsov and his officers. He was afraid of everything, even that he would be seized, fettered and exiled to Siberia or simply killed, and so was on his guard.

He asked Eldar, who came to see him, where his followers had been put, where the horses were, and whether they had had their weapons taken away.

Eldar informed him that the horses were in the Prince's stable, the men had been put in a barn, their weapons had been left with them, and the interpreter had been bringing them food and tea.

Perplexed, Hadji Murat shook his head and, after getting undressed, took up the position for prayer. When he had finished, he ordered his silver dagger to be brought to him and, having dressed and put on his belt, he sat with his legs up on an ottoman to wait and see what would happen.

After four o'clock he was summoned to have lunch with the Prince.

At lunch Hadji Murat ate nothing except some pilau, which he took for himself from the same place from which Maria Vasilyevna had helped herself.

'He's afraid we might poison him,' said Maria Vasilyevna to her husband. 'He took from where I took.' And she turned straight away to Hadji Murat, asking him through the interpreter when he would now be praying again. Hadji Murat raised five fingers and pointed at the sun.

'Soon, then.'

Vorontsov took out his Breguet and pressed the mainspring – the watch struck four and one quarter. Hadji Murat was obviously surprised by this chiming and he asked him to ring it again and to look at the watch.

'*Voilà l'occasion. Donnez-lui la montre,*'⁵ said Maria Vasilyevna to her husband.

Vorontsov immediately offered the watch to Hadji Murat. Hadji Murat put his hand to his chest and took the watch. He pressed the mainspring several times, listened, and shook his head approvingly.

After lunch Meller-Zakomelsky's adjutant was announced to the Prince.

The adjutant told the Prince that, when he learnt about Hadji Murat's surrender, the general was very displeased that he had not been informed about it, and that he demanded Hadji Murat be delivered up to him at once. Vorontsov said that the general's order would be carried out and, after conveying the general's demand to Hadji Murat through the interpreter, he asked him to go with him to Meller.

When Maria Vasilyevna learnt why the adjutant had come, she immediately realised that there could be trouble between her husband and the general and, despite all her husband's arguments, she got ready to go to see the general together with him and Hadji Murat.

'*Vous feriez bien mieux de rester; c'est mon affaire, non pas la votre.*'

'*Vous ne pouvez pas m'empêcher d'aller voir madame la générale.*'[76]

'You could do that at another time.'

'But I want to go now.'

There was nothing for it. Vorontsov consented, and all three of them went.

When they arrived, Meller escorted Maria Vasilyevna to his wife with gloomy courtesy, while ordering the adjutant to escort Hadji Murat into the reception room and not to let him out anywhere until told.

'Please,' he said to Vorontsov, opening the door into his study and letting the Prince in ahead of him.

On entering the study he stopped in front of the Prince and, without asking him to sit down, said:

'I am the military commander here, and for that reason all negotiations with the enemy should be conducted through me. Why did you not inform me of Hadji Murat's surrender?'

'A scout came to me and announced Hadji Murat's desire to hand himself over to me,' replied Vorontsov, turning pale in his agitation, expecting a rude outburst from the enraged general, and at the same time becoming infected with his rage.

'I'm asking why you didn't inform me?'

'I intended to do so, Baron, but –'

'I'm not "Baron" to you, but "Your Excellency".'

And at this point the baron's long-contained irritation burst out. He voiced everything that had long been boiling up inside him.

'I haven't been serving my sovereign for twenty-seven years so that people who began their service only yesterday, using their family connections, can deal with things that don't concern them under my very nose.'

'Your Excellency! Please don't say things that are unjust,' Vorontsov interrupted him.

'I'm speaking the truth and I won't allow –' began the general in even greater irritation.

At this moment Maria Vasilyevna came in with her skirts rustling, and after her a tall, modest lady, Meller-Zakomelsky's wife.

'Now that's enough, Baron. Simon did not mean to cause you any trouble,' began Maria Vasilyevna.

'It's not that I'm speaking of, Princess…'

'You know, it'd be better if we dropped this. You know what they say: "a bad scrap is better than a good quarrel"[7]. Oh, what am I saying…' She burst out laughing.

And the angry general submitted to the enchanting smile of the beauty. Beneath his moustache there was a glimpse of a smile.

'I admit that I was wrong,' said Vorontsov, 'but –'

'Well and I did get a little heated,' said Meller, and offered his hand to the Prince.

Peace was established, and it was decided to leave Hadji Murat with Meller for a time, and then to send him to the commander of the left flank.

Hadji Murat sat in the room next door and, although he did not understand what they were saying, he did understand what he needed to understand: that they were arguing about him, and that his leaving Shamil was a matter of enormous importance for the Russians, and that for this reason, if only they did not exile or kill him, he would be able to demand a lot from them. Apart from that he also realised that Meller-Zakomelsky, although he was the commander, did not have the significance that Vorontsov, his subordinate, did, and that Vorontsov was important, and that Meller-Zakomelsky was not important; and so, when Meller-Zakomelsky summoned Hadji Murat and began questioning him, Hadji Murat bore himself proudly and solemnly, saying that he had come out of the mountains in order to serve the white Tsar, and that he would give an account of everything only to his chief, that is to the commander-in-chief, Prince Vorontsov, in Tiflis.

7

The wounded Avdeyev was brought to the hospital, which was located in a small, boarded building on the way out of the fortress, and he was put on one of the empty beds in the open ward. There were four patients in the ward: one with typhus, who was tossing and turning in a fever, another with blue shadows under his eyes, feverish, expecting a paroxysm and constantly yawning, and two others who had been wounded in a raid three weeks before, one in the wrist (he was on his feet), the other in the shoulder (he was sitting on his bed). All of them except the one with typhus surrounded the man who was carried in and questioned those who had brought him.

'Another time they'll be shooting away like they were chucking peas at you and everything's fine, whereas here they only fired about half a dozen times,' said one of those who had brought him.

'Depends on your luck!'

'Ouch,' cried Avdeyev loudly, holding back the pain, when they set about putting him on the bed. And when they had put him on it, he frowned and did not groan any more, but merely shifted the soles of his feet continually. He held the wound with his hands and looked fixedly ahead.

The doctor came and ordered the wounded man to be turned over to see whether the bullet had come out at the back.

'And what's this?' asked the doctor, indicating the criss-crossing white weals on his back and bottom.

'That's old stuff, Your Honour,' croaked Avdeyev.

They were the scars of his punishment for spending money on drink.

Avdeyev was turned back over again, and the doctor spent a long time digging around in his stomach with a probe and groping for the bullet, but he could not get it out. After bandaging the wound and sealing it with sticking plaster, the doctor left. All the time he was digging in the wound and bandaging it, Avdeyev lay with gritted teeth and closed eyes. But when the doctor had gone away, he opened his eyes and looked around himself in surprise. His eyes were directed at the patients and the doctor's assistant, yet it was as if he did not see them, but saw something else that very much surprised him.

Avdeyev's comrades came, Panov and Seryogin. Avdeyev continued lying in just the same way, gazing ahead of himself in surprise. He could not recognise his comrades for a long time, despite the fact that his eyes were looking straight at them.

'Pyotra, do you want anything to be sent home?' asked Panov.

Avdeyev did not reply, even though he was looking into Panov's face.

'I'm saying, do you want anything to be sent home?' asked Panov again, touching his cold, big-boned hand.

Avdeyev seemed to come round.

'Ah, Antonych is here?'

'Yes, Here I am. Do you want anything to be sent home? Seryogin'll write it.'

'Seryogin,' said Avdeyev, transferring his eyes to Seryogin with difficulty, 'will you write?... Well then, notify them: "Your son, your Petrukha, has passed away." I envied my brother. I was telling you just today. Only now, well, I'm glad. Just let him live. God grant him, I'm glad. You write that.'

After saying this he was silent for a long time with his eyes fixed on Panov.

'Well, did you find the pipe?' he suddenly asked.

Panov shook his head and did not reply.

'The pipe, the pipe, I'm saying, did you find it?' repeated Avdeyev.

'It was in my bag.'

'There you are. Well give me a candle now, I'll be dying soon,' said Avdeyev.

At this moment Poltoratsky arrived to pay his soldier a visit.

'Well, old fellow, bad, is it?' he said.

Avdeyev closed his eyes and shook his head to say no. His face with its prominent cheek-bones was pale and severe. He made no reply and only repeated once more, turning to Panov:

'Give me a candle. I'm going to die.'

A candle was put in his hand, but his fingers would not bend, so it was put between his fingers and held there. Poltoratsky left, and five minutes after his departure the doctor's assistant put his ear to Avdeyev's heart and said that he was dead.

In the communiqué that was sent to Tiflis, Avdeyev's death was described in the following way: 'On the 23rd of November two companies of the Kurinsky Regiment marched out of the fortress to fell trees. In the middle of the day a significant gathering of mountaineers suddenly attacked the woodcutters. The line began to withdraw, and at this point the Second Company attacked with bayonets and overran the mountaineers. Two privates were slightly wounded in the action and one was killed, while the mountaineers lost about one hundred men, dead and wounded.'

8

On that very day when Petrukha Avdeyev was dying in the hospital in Vozdvizhenskaya, his aged father, the wife of the brother in whose place he had become a soldier, and the daughter of his elder brother, a young girl of marriageable age, were threshing oats on a frosty threshing-floor. Deep snow had fallen the day before and by morning it had become very icy. The old man was already awake with the third cock-crow and, seeing the bright light of the moon at the frosted window, he climbed off the stove, put on his boots, dressed in his fur coat and hat and went to the threshing-floor. After a couple of hours' work there the old man returned to the hut and woke his son and the women. When the woman and the girl arrived at the threshing-floor it had been cleared, a wooden spade stood upright in the fine white snow with, alongside it, a brush with the bristles uppermost, and the sheaves of oats were laid out in two rows, stalk by stalk, in a long line across the clear threshing-floor. They sorted out the flails and began threshing, working together rhythmically with their three blows. The old man struck hard with a heavy flail, breaking up the straw, the girl struck from above with a flat blow, his daughter-in-law turned the oats aside.

The moon went down and it began to get light; and they were already finishing the line when the elder son, Akim, came out to join the workers in a short fur coat and hat.

'What are you doing, lazing around?' his father shouted at him, stopping threshing and leaning on his flail.

'Someone needs to see to the horses.'

'See to the horses,' his father mimicked him. 'The old woman'll see to them. Get a flail. You're much too fat. Drunkard!'

'You didn't give me the drink though, did you?' muttered the son.

'What was that?' asked the old man threateningly, frowning and missing a blow.

The son picked up a flail, and the work went on with four flails: trap, ta-pa-tap, trap, ta-pa-tap... Trap! – the heavy flail of the old man would strike every fourth blow.

'Look at the back of his neck, like it belonged to a master. My trousers don't keep like that,' said the old man, missing his blow and just turning the end of the flail over in the air so as not to lose the rhythm.

They finished the line and the women began removing the straw with rakes.

'Petrukha was a fool to go instead of you. They'd have knocked some sense into you as a soldier, and he was worth five of the likes of you at home.'

'Come on, that's enough, Dad,' said the daughter-in-law, throwing aside the broken bindings.

'Yes, feed the six of you, but there's no work out of any of you. Petrukha used to do the work of two himself, not like...'

Along the trodden-down path from the yard, crunching over the snow in new bast shoes over tightly bound woollen puttees, came the old woman. The men raked the unwinnowed grain together into a pile, the women and the girl swept up.

'The village elder's been in. Everyone's to take bricks to the master's,' said the old woman. 'I've got breakfast ready. Are you going then?'

'Alright. Harness the roan and off you go,' said the old man to Akim. 'And see that I don't have to answer for you like the other day. You think of Petrukha.'

'When he was at home he was told off,' Akim now snapped at his father, 'and now, as he's not here, you have a go at me.'

'You must deserve it then,' said his mother, just as angrily. 'You're no exchange for Petrukha.'

'Oh alright!' said the son.

'That's just it: alright. The flour's gone on drink, and now you say: alright.'

'Let sleeping dogs lie,' said the daughter-in-law, and, laying down their flails, they set off towards the house.

Disagreements between father and son had begun long ago, almost from the time Pyotr had been sent away to the army. Even then the old man had felt that he had exchanged a cuckoo for a hawk. It was true that according to the law, as the old man understood it, the childless one had to go instead of the one with a family. Akim had four children, Pyotr had nobody, but Pyotr was a worker, just like his father: deft, quick-witted, strong, robust and, most important, hard-working. He was always working. If he was passing by people working, he would immediately offer to help, just as his father used to do – either he would work a row or two with a scythe, or load a cart, or cut down a tree, or chop some firewood. The old man was sorry for him, but there was nothing for it. Soldiering was like death. A soldier was out on his own, and there was no point in thinking about him and torturing your soul. Only from time to time did the old man reminisce about him, like today, to irritate his elder son. Whereas his mother often thought about her younger son and had been asking the old man for a long time now, over a year, to send Petrukha a little money. But the old man said nothing in reply.

The Avdeyev household was well-off, and the old man had a little money hidden away, but not for anything would he have thought of touching what had been saved. Now, when the old woman heard him mentioning his younger son, she decided to ask him again to send their son even just a rouble when the oats were sold. She did just that. Remaining alone with the old man when the youngsters went off to the master's to work, she persuaded her husband to send a rouble to Petrukha out of the oats money. So that when from the winnowed piles twelve quarters of oats were tipped onto pieces of sacking in three sledges and the sacking was neatly fastened up with wooden pegs, she gave the old man a letter, written at her dictation by the sexton, and the old man promised to attach a rouble to the letter in town and send it off.

The old man took the letter and put it away in his purse, and after a prayer to God, dressed in his new fur coat and caftan and in clean white woollen puttees, he got into the first sledge and set off for town. His grandson was in the third sledge. In town the old man asked a yardman to read the letter to him, and listened to it attentively and approvingly.

In Petrukha's mother's letter there was, firstly, a blessing, secondly, greetings from everyone, news of the death of his godfather, and towards the end news about how Aksinya (Pyotr's wife) 'no longer wanted to live with us and left home. She's said to be living a good and honest life.' There was mention of the gift, the rouble, and in addition there was what the saddened old woman, with tears in her eyes, had asked the sexton to write word for word, directly from her:

'What's more, my sweet child, my dear Petrushenka, I've cried my old eyes out in grieving over you. My darling ray of sunshine, who have you left me with…' At this point the old woman had begun to howl, had burst into tears and said:

'That'll do.'

And so it remained in the letter, but Petrukha was not destined to receive either this news about his wife leaving home, or the rouble, or his mother's final words. This letter and the money came back with the news that Petrukha had been killed in the war, 'defending the Tsar, his homeland and the Orthodox faith'. That was what the military clerk wrote.

When the old woman received this news she lamented while she had the time, and then got on with her work. And on the first Sunday she went to church and handed out pieces of holy bread 'to the good people, in remembrance of God's servant, Pyotr'.

The soldier's wife, Aksinya, lamented too when she learnt of the death 'of the beloved husband, with whom' she 'had lived just one short year'. She felt pity for her husband and the whole of her ruined life. And in her lamentation she remembered 'Pyotr Mikhailovich's light-brown curls, and his love' and her 'bitter life with little orphaned Ivan', and she bitterly rebuked 'Petrusha for taking pity on his brother and not taking pity on a bitter woman, a wanderer among strangers'.

But in the depths of her soul Aksinya was pleased at Pyotr's death. She was pregnant again by the shop assistant she lived with, and now nobody could abuse her any more, and the shop assistant could marry her, as he told her he would when he was persuading her to make love.

9

Mikhail Semyonovich Vorontsov, brought up in England, son of the Russian ambassador, was, among senior Russian officials, a man of European education rare for that time, ambitious, kind and gentle in his manner with inferiors and a subtle courtier in his relations with superiors. He could not understand a life without power and without obedience. He held all the highest ranks and decorations and was considered a skilled soldier, the victor over Napoleon even at Craonne[8]. In 1851 he was over seventy years old, but he was still very fresh, he moved briskly and, most importantly, he was in full possession of all the agility of a subtle and genial mind, which was focussed on sustaining his power and ensuring and spreading his popularity. He enjoyed great wealth – both his own and that of his wife, Countess Branitskaya – and a huge income in his capacity as governor-general, and he spent the greater part of his means on laying out a palace and garden on the southern shore of the Crimea.

On the evening of the 7th of December 1851 a courier's troika drove up to his palace in Tiflis. The officer, tired and completely black with dust, who had brought from General Kozlovsky the news of Hadji Murat's surrender to the Russians, flexed his legs and walked past the sentries into the wide porch of the governor-general's palace. It was six o'clock in the evening, and Vorontsov was on his way to dinner when the arrival of the courier was reported to him. Vorontsov received the courier without delay, and so was a few minutes late for dinner. When he entered the drawing-room, the thirty or so dinner guests sitting near Princess Elizaveta Xavierevna and standing in groups by the windows rose and turned to face the man who had come in. Vorontsov was wearing his usual black military frock-coat without epaulettes, but with shoulder-straps, and a white cross around his neck. His clean-shaven vulpine face was smiling pleasantly, and his eyes narrowed, surveying the assembled company.

On entering the drawing-room with soft, rapid steps, he apologised to the ladies for being late, greeted the men and went up to the Georgian Princess Manana Orbeliani, a tall, plump, forty-five-year-old beauty of oriental stamp, and offered his arm to lead her to the table. Princess Elizaveta Xavierevna herself offered her hand to a visiting general with rather red hair and a bristling moustache. A Georgian prince offered his arm to Countess Choiseuil, a friend of the Princess. Dr Andreyevsky, the adjutants and the rest, some with ladies, some without ladies, followed on behind the three couples. Footmen in caftans, stockings and shoes drew the chairs back, then up to the table for those taking their seats; the head waiter solemnly served steaming soup from a silver tureen.

Vorontsov sat down in the middle of the long table. Opposite him sat the Princess, his wife, with the general. To his right was his lady, the beautiful Orbeliani, to his left – an elegant, black-haired, rosy, young Georgian princess in brilliant jewellery who smiled incessantly.

'*Excellentes, chère amie,*' responded Vorontsov to the Princess' question about what news he had received from the courier. '*Simon a eu de la chance.*'[9]

And in such a way that all those seated at the table could hear, he began to recount the astonishing news – for him alone was it not entirely news, because negotiations had been under way for a long time – about how Shamil's renowned, most courageous aide, Hadji Murat, had handed himself over to the Russians and would be brought to Tiflis any day now.

All the diners, even the junior ones, the adjutants and officials sitting at the far end of the table who had hitherto been quietly laughing about something, all fell silent and listened.

'And have you, General, met this Hadji Murat?' the Princess asked her neighbour, the red-haired general with the bristling moustache, when the Prince stopped speaking.

'More than once, Princess.'

And the general told of how in 1843, after the mountaineers had taken Gergebil, Hadji Murat had chanced upon General Passek's detachment, and how he had killed Colonel Zolotukhin almost before their very eyes.

Vorontsov listened to the general with a pleasant smile, obviously pleased that the general had begun to talk freely. But suddenly Vorontsov's face took on an absent-minded and melancholy expression.

The freely talking general had begun telling about where he had come across Hadji Murat the second time.

'For it was he,' said the general, 'you'll be so good as to recall, Your Highness, that organised the ambush on the rescue in the Sukhar expedition.'

'Where?' Vorontsov queried him, narrowing his eyes.

The thing was, what the bold general was calling 'the rescue' was the affair in the ill-starred Dargo campaign in which an entire detachment under the command of Prince Vorontsov would certainly have perished if it had not been rescued by newly arrived troops. Everyone was aware that the whole Dargo campaign under Vorontsov's leadership, in which the Russians lost many dead and wounded and several cannon, was a shameful episode, and so if anybody did speak about that campaign in

Vorontsov's presence, it was only in the terms in which Vorontsov wrote his report to the Tsar, namely that it was a brilliant feat of Russian arms. But the use of the word 'rescue' was a direct indication of the fact that it was not a brilliant feat, but an error that had doomed many men. Everybody understood this, and some pretended not to notice the significance of the general's words, others anxiously awaited what would happen next; some smiled and exchanged glances.

Only the red-haired general with the bristling moustache noticed nothing and, carried away by his story, he calmly replied:

'On the rescue, Your Highness.'

And once started on a favourite topic, the general gave a detailed account of how 'this Hadji Murat cut the detachment in two so cleverly that, had no one come to our rescue,' – he seemed to repeat the word 'rescue' particularly lovingly – 'we would all have stayed there, because –'

The general did not manage to finish all he had to say because Manana Orbeliani, realising what was wrong, interrupted the general's speech by questioning him about the comfort of his accommodation in Tiflis. The general glanced around at everyone in surprise and at his adjutant, who was giving him a fixed and meaningful look from the end of the table – and suddenly he understood. Without answering the Princess, he frowned, fell silent and began hurriedly eating, without chewing, the refined dish, incomprehensible to him in appearance and even taste, that lay on his plate.

Everyone felt awkward, but the awkwardness of the situation was righted by the Georgian prince, a very stupid man, but an unusually subtle and skilful flatterer and courtier, who was sitting on the other side of Princess Vorontsova. As if noticing nothing, he began telling in a loud voice of how Hadji Murat had kidnapped the widow of Akhmet Khan of Mekhtula.

'He entered the settlement at night, seized what he needed and galloped off with the whole lot.'

'And why did he need this woman in particular?' asked the Princess.

'He and her husband were enemies, he'd been after him, but hadn't managed to meet up with him anywhere right up till his death, and so he avenged himself on the widow.'

The Princess translated this into French for her old friend Countess Choiseul who was sitting next to the Georgian prince.

'*Quel horreur!*'[10] said the Countess, closing her eyes and shaking her head.

'Oh no,' said Vorontsov with a smile, 'I'm told that he treated his captive with chivalrous respect and later released her.'

'Yes, in exchange for a ransom.'

'Well naturally, but nonetheless he acted honourably.'

These words from the Prince set the tone for the subsequent stories about Hadji Murat. The courtiers understood that the greater the significance ascribed to Hadji Murat, the more pleasant it would be for Prince Vorontsov.

'This man has astonishing courage. A remarkable man.'

'Of course, in '49 he burst into Temir-Khan-Shura in broad daylight and looted the shops.'

An Armenian sitting at the end of the table, who had been in Temir-Khan-Shura at the time, recounted the details of this exploit of Hadji Murat's.

And in general, the entire dinner passed with stories about Hadji Murat. They all vied with one another in praising his courage, intelligence, magnanimity. Somebody told of how he had ordered twenty-six prisoners to be killed, but even this met with the usual response:

'What can one do! *À la guerre comme à la guerre*[11].'

'He's a major figure.'

'If he'd been born in Europe, perhaps he'd have been a new Napoleon,' said the stupid Georgian prince who had the gift for flattery.

He knew that any mention of Napoleon, for victory over whom Vorontsov wore the white cross around his neck, was pleasing to the Prince.

'Well, maybe not Napoleon, but a dashing cavalry general – yes,' said Vorontsov.

'If not Napoleon, then Murat[12].'

'And his name is Hadji Murat.'

'Hadji Murat's surrendered, now it's the end for Shamil too,' said somebody.

'They can sense that *now*' (this '*now*' meant: 'faced by Vorontsov') 'they can't hold out.'

'*Tout cela est grâce à vous*,'[13] said Manana Orbeliani.

Prince Vorontsov tried to contain the waves of flattery which were already beginning to drown him. But it was pleasant for him, and he led his lady from the table into the drawing-room in the very best frame of mind.

After dinner, while coffee was being taken round in the drawing-room, the Prince was especially nice with everyone, and, going up to the general with the bristling red moustache, he tried to show him that he had not noticed his awkwardness.

When he had gone round to all the guests, he sat down to play cards. He only played the old game of ombre. The Prince's partners were the Georgian prince, then an Armenian general who had learnt to play ombre from the Prince's valet, and the fourth was Dr Andreyevsky, renowned for his power.

Placing a gold snuffbox with a portrait of Alexander I beside him, Vorontsov tore open a pack of satin cards and was going to lay them out, when in came his valet, an Italian, Giovanni, with a letter on a silver tray.

'Another courier, Your Highness.'

Vorontsov put the cards down and, with an apology, broke the seal and began to read.

The letter was from his son. He described how Hadji Murat had come over and the clash with Meller-Zakomelsky.

The Princess came up and asked what their son wrote.

'Still the same business. He had some disagreements with the commander of the fortress. *Simon a eu tort. But all's well that ends well*,'[14] he added, handing the letter to his wife, and, turning to his partners, who had been waiting politely, he invited them to take up the cards.

When the first hand had been dealt, Vorontsov opened his snuffbox and did what he was wont to do when in a particularly good frame of mind: with his white hands, wrinkled by age, he took out a pinch of French snuff, brought it up to his nose and scattered it out.

10

When Hadji Murat came to see Vorontsov on the next day, the Prince's reception room was full of people. The general with the bristling moustache of the day before was here, wearing full uniform and decorations, come to take his leave; here too was a regimental commander who was threatened with trial over abuses in the provisioning of his regiment; here was a rich Armenian, a protégé of Dr Andreyevsky, who held the rights to vodka-farming and was now soliciting a renewal of the contract; here, all in black, was the widow of an officer who had been killed, come to ask for a pension or to have her children raised at the expense of the government; here was a bankrupt Georgian prince in a magnificent Georgian costume, looking to obtain a former church estate for himself; here was a police officer with a large package in which was a plan for a new method of subjugating the Caucasus; here was a khan who had only come so that he could tell people at home that he had been received by the Prince.

They all awaited their turn, and one by one they were led by a handsome, fair-haired young adjutant into the Prince's office.

When Hadji Murat entered the reception room at a brisk pace, limping slightly, all eyes turned on him, and he heard his name pronounced in a whisper in various corners.

Hadji Murat was dressed in a long white Circassian coat over a brown quilted jacket with fine silver galloon on the collar. On his legs and feet he wore black leggings and similar slippers that fitted tightly round his soles like a glove; on his head – a sheepskin hat and turban, that very turban because of which, following Akhmet Khan's denunciation, he was arrested by General Klugenau, and which was the reason for his going over to Shamil. Hadji Murat stepped quickly over the parquet of the reception room with his whole slender figure rocking a little owing to a slight limp in one leg, which was shorter than the other. His wide-set eyes gazed calmly ahead and seemed not to see anyone.

The handsome adjutant greeted Hadji Murat and asked him to take a seat while he reported to the Prince. But Hadji Murat refused to sit down and, putting his hands behind his dagger, he continued to stand with his legs set apart, surveying those in attendance with contempt.

The interpreter, Prince Tarkhanov, went up to Hadji Murat and began speaking to him. Hadji Murat replied unwillingly, abruptly. From the office there emerged a Kumyk prince who had made a complaint about a police officer, and after him the adjutant called Hadji Murat, led him up to the door of the office and let him through.

Vorontsov received Hadji Murat standing by the edge of his desk. The old white face of the commander-in-chief was not so smiling as it had been the day before, but was rather stern and solemn.

Upon entering the large room with its huge desk and large green-curtained windows, Hadji Murat put his small, tanned hands to the point on his chest where the white Circassian coat-breasts crossed and, with his eyes lowered, said unhurriedly, distinctly and respectfully in the Kumyk dialect he spoke so well:

'I hand myself over into the exalted protection of the great Tsar and you. I promise faithfully to serve the white Tsar to my last drop of blood and hope to be of use in the war with Shamil, my enemy and yours.'

When he had heard the interpreter out, Vorontsov looked at Hadji Murat, and Hadji Murat looked into the face of Vorontsov.

When the eyes of these two men met, they told one another much that was inexpressible in words, and not at all what was said by the interpreter. They told directly, without words, the whole truth about one another: Vorontsov's eyes said that he did not believe a single word of all that Hadji Murat had said, that he knew he was the enemy of everything Russian and would always remain so, and was submitting now only because he had been forced into it. And Hadji Murat understood this and nonetheless attested to his loyalty. And Hadji Murat's eyes said that this old man ought to be thinking about death, not about war, but that although he was old, still he was cunning, and one needed to be cautious with him. And Vorontsov understood this and nonetheless said to Hadji Murat what he considered necessary for the success of the war.

'Tell him,' said Vorontsov to the interpreter in the familiar way he used with young officers, 'that our sovereign is just as gracious as he is mighty and will at my request doubtless forgive him and accept him into his service. Have you conveyed that?' he asked, looking at Hadji Murat. 'And until I receive the gracious decision of my ruler, tell him that I take it upon myself to receive him and make his stay with us a pleasant one.'

Hadji Murat once again pressed his hands to the middle of his chest and began animatedly saying something.

He said, as the interpreter conveyed it, that even before, when he ruled Avaria in 1839, he had served the Russians faithfully, and would never have betrayed them but for his enemy, Akhmet Khan, who wanted to destroy him and had slandered him before General Klugenau.

'I know, I know,' said Vorontsov (although if he had known, he had in any event forgotten all this long ago). 'I know,' he said, sitting down and indicating to Hadji Murat the ottoman standing by the wall. But Hadji Murat would not sit down, shrugging his powerful shoulders to signify that he could not bring himself to be seated in the presence of such an important man.

'Both Akhmet Khan and Shamil, both are my enemies,' he continued, turning to the interpreter. 'Tell the Prince: Akhmet Khan is dead, I could not take revenge on him, but Shamil is still alive, and I shall not die until I have repaid him,' he said, furrowing his brow and firmly clenching his jaw.

'Yes, yes,' pronounced Vorontsov, calmly. 'And how does he want to repay Shamil?' he said to the interpreter. 'And tell him that he can sit down.'

Hadji Murat again refused to sit down, and to the question conveyed to him he replied that the reason he had surrendered to the Russians was in order to help them to destroy Shamil.

'Good, good,' said Vorontsov. 'And what precisely does he want to do? Sit down, sit down…'

Hadji Murat sat down and said that if only he were sent to the Lezghian line and given a body of troops, he would guarantee to raise the whole of Dagestan, and Shamil would not be able to survive.

'That's good. That's a possibility,' said Vorontsov. 'I will consider it.'

The interpreter conveyed Vorontsov's words to Hadji Murat. Hadji Murat fell into thought.

'Tell the chief,' he added, 'that my family is in the hands of my enemy; and until my family is in the mountains, I am tied and cannot serve. He will kill my wife, he will kill my mother, he will kill my children if I go directly against him. Let the Prince only rescue my family, exchange prisoners for them, and then I shall either die or I shall destroy Shamil.'

'Good, good,' said Vorontsov. 'We'll think about it. But now let him go to the chief of staff and set out for him in detail his position, his intentions and wishes.'

Thus ended Hadji Murat's first meeting with Vorontsov.

That same day, in the evening, in the new theatre, decorated in the oriental taste, there appeared the conspicuous figure of the limping Hadji Murat in his turban. He came in with Vorontsov's adjutant, Loris-Melikov, who had been appointed to look after him, and took his place in the front row. After sitting through the first act with oriental, Muslim dignity, not only without any expression of surprise, but with a look of indifference, Hadji Murat rose and, calmly surveying the audience, left, attracting the attention of the whole audience.

The next day was a Monday, the evening when the Vorontsovs usually entertained. In the large, brightly lit reception hall, music was coming from a source unseen in the winter garden. Women, young and not so very young, in clothes that revealed both their necks and their arms, and almost their breasts, twirled in the embraces of men in bright dress uniform. By the mountain of the buffet footmen in red tailcoats, stockings and shoes poured champagne and carried sweets around to the ladies. The wife of the chief, similarly half-naked, despite her years, walked among the guests, smiling amicably, and said a few kind words through the interpreter to Hadji Murat, who was surveying the guests with the same indifference as the day before at the theatre. After the hostess, other naked women also came up to Hadji Murat, and all, without any shame, stood in front of him and, smiling, kept asking him one and the same thing: how he liked what he saw. Vorontsov himself, in gold epaulettes and aiguillettes with a white cross around his neck and a sash, went up to him and asked the same thing, obviously certain, like all those who asked, that Hadji Murat could not but like everything that he saw. And Hadji Murat replied to Vorontsov too as he replied to everyone: that *they* did not have this – without saying whether it was a good thing or a bad thing that they did not have it.

Hadji Murat tried to start a conversation with Vorontsov here too, at the ball, about the matter of the ransom of his family, but Vorontsov pretended that he did not hear his words and walked away from him. And Loris-Melikov said later on to Hadji Murat that this was not the place to talk about business.

When it struck eleven o'clock and Hadji Murat checked the time on his watch, presented to him by Maria Vasilyevna, he asked Loris-Melikov if he could leave. Loris-Melikov said that he could, but that it would be better to stay. Despite this, Hadji Murat did not stay, and left in the phaeton that had been put at his disposal for the apartment that had been assigned to him.

11

On the fifth day of Hadji Murat's stay in Tiflis, Loris-Melikov, the governor-general's adjutant, went to see him on the instructions of the commander-in-chief.

'Both my head and my hands are glad to be of service to the chief,' said Hadji Murat, with his customary diplomatic expression, bowing his head and putting his hands to his chest. 'Give me my orders,' he said, gazing amicably into Loris-Melikov's eyes.

Loris-Melikov sat down in the armchair that stood by the table, Hadji Murat sank onto the low ottoman opposite him and, resting his hands on his knees, bowed his head and began to listen carefully to what Loris-Melikov was saying to him. Loris-Melikov, who spoke Tatar fluently, said that the Prince, although he knew about Hadji Murat's past, wanted to learn the whole of his story from him himself.

'You tell me,' said Loris-Melikov, 'and I'll write it down, then I'll translate it into Russian, and the Prince will send it to the sovereign.'

Hadji Murat was silent for a moment (not only did he never interrupt anyone's speech, but he always waited to see whether the person speaking would say something more), then he raised his head, shook back his sheepskin hat, and smiled that particular, childlike smile with which he had already captivated Maria Vasilyevna.

'That can be done,' he said, obviously flattered by the idea that his story would be read by the sovereign.

'Tell me everything from the beginning, without hurrying,' said Loris-Melikov, with the informality characteristic of Tatar, taking his notebook from his pocket.

'That can be done, only there is a great deal, a very great deal to tell. A lot of things have happened,' said Hadji Murat.

'If you don't have time in one day, you can finish the story another day,' said Loris-Melikov.

'Shall I begin at the beginning?'

'Yes, at the very beginning: where you were born, where you lived.'

Hadji Murat lowered his head and sat like that for a long time; then he picked up a stick that was lying by the ottoman, took out from under his dagger with its ivory handle set in gold a small, razor-sharp, damask steel knife and began whittling the stick with it and talking at one and the same time:

'Write: I was born in Tselmes, a small village the size of an ass's head, as we say in the mountains,' he began. 'Not far from us, two gunshots away, was Khunzakh where the khans lived. And our family was close to them. My mother fed the elder khan, Abununtsal Khan, and because of that I became close to the khans. There were three khans: Abununtsal Khan, my brother Osman's foster-brother, Umma Khan, my sworn brother, and Bulach Khan, the youngest, the one that Shamil threw off a cliff. But that is later on. I was about fifteen when followers of Muridism[15] started going round the villages. They struck the rocks with wooden sabres and shouted: "Muslims, Holy War!" The Chechens all went over to these men and the Avars began to go across to them. At that time I lived in the palace. I was like a brother to the khans: I did what I wanted and became rich. I had both horses and weapons, and I had money. I lived for my own pleasure and did not think about a thing. And I lived like that until the time when Kazi Mullah was killed[16], and Gamzat took his place. Gamzat sent envoys to the khans to say that if they did not accept the Holy War, he would sack Khunzakh. Now they had to think. The khans were afraid of the Russians, afraid of accepting the Holy War, and the khans' mother sent me with her son, the second one, Umma Khan, to Tiflis, to ask for help against Gamzat from the Russian chief. The chief was Rozen, the baron. He would not receive either me or Umma Khan. He had us told that he would help, and he did nothing. Only his officers started visiting us and playing cards with Umma Khan. They gave him wine to drink and took him to bad places, and he lost all he had to them at cards. In body he was strong as an ox, and brave as a lion, but he was weak as water in spirit. He would have lost our last horses and weapons if I had not taken him away. After Tiflis my ideas changed, and I began trying to persuade the khans' mother and the young khans to accept the Holy War.'

'Why was it your ideas changed?' asked Loris-Melikov, 'didn't you like the Russians?'

Hadji Murat was silent for a moment.

'No, I did not,' he said decisively, and closed his eyes. 'And there was another business that made me want to accept the Holy War.'

'What business was that?'

'Near Tselmes the khan and I clashed with three followers of Muridism: two got away, but the third I killed with my pistol. When I went up to him to take off his weapons he was still alive. He looked at me. "You," he said, "have killed me. That is good for me. But you are a Muslim, both young and strong: accept the Holy War. It is God's will."'

'Well and you accepted it?'

'I did not accept it, but I started thinking,' said Hadji Murat, and continued his tale. 'When Gamzat approached Khunzakh we sent the old men out to him and told them to say that we agreed to accept the Holy War, if only he would send a learned man to us to explain how it was to be conducted. Gamzat ordered the old men's moustaches to be shaved off, their nostrils pierced, flat cakes to be hung from their noses, and had them sent back. The old men said that Gamzat was prepared to send us a sheikh to teach us Holy War, but only on condition that the khans' mother send him her youngest son as a hostage. The khans' mother had trust and sent Bulach Khan to Gamzat. Gamzat received Bulach Khan well and sent men to us to invite the elder brothers to stay with him too. He ordered them to say that he wanted to serve the khans just as his father had served their father. The khans' mother was a weak, stupid and insolent woman, like all women when they live according to their own will. She was afraid to send both sons and sent only Umma Khan. I went with him. Gamzat's followers met us a kilometre away, and they sang, and fired their rifles, and performed riding tricks around us. And when we rode up, Gamzat came out of his tent, came up to Umma Khan's stirrup, and received him as a khan. He said: "I have done no harm to your house and do not wish to do any. Only do not kill me and do not prevent me from bringing men to Holy War. And I shall serve you with all my troops as my father served your father. Allow me to live in your house. I shall help you with my advice, and you do as you wish." Umma Khan was slow-witted in speech. He did not know what to say and was silent. Then I said that if that was the case, then let Gamzat go to Khunzakh. The khans' mother and the khan would receive him with honour. But I was not allowed to finish, and here for the first time I clashed with Shamil. He was there too, alongside the imam. "It is not you being asked, but the khan," he said to me. I fell silent, and Gamzat led Umma Khan into his tent. Then Gamzat called me and asked me to ride with his envoys to Khunzakh. I went. The envoys began persuading the khans' mother to let the eldest khan go to Gamzat too. I saw treachery and told the khans' mother not to send her son. But a woman has as much sense in her head as there are hairs on an egg. The khans' mother had trust and told her son to go. Abununtsal did not want to. Then she said: "You are obviously afraid." She knew, like a bee, where the sting would hurt him most. Abununtsal flared up, did not even consider replying, and ordered horses to be saddled. I went with him. Gamzat greeted us even better than he had Umma Khan. He rode out to meet us himself two gunshots down the mountain. Horsemen with pennants rode behind him singing "*Lya illyakha il Allah*", shooting and performing riding tricks. When we rode up to the camp, Gamzat led the khan into his tent. And I stayed with the horses. I was down the hill when shooting began inside Gamzat's tent. I ran up to the tent. Umma Khan was lying face down in a pool of blood, while Abununtsal was struggling with Gamzat's followers. Half his face had been chopped off and was hanging loose. He had taken hold of it with one hand, and with the other he was hacking with his dagger at anyone who came close to him. While I was there he cut down one of Gamzat's brothers and had already turned to strike another, but at this point Gamzat's followers began shooting at him and he fell.'

Hadji Murat stopped, his tanned face turned a deep red and his eyes filled with blood.

'Fear came upon me and I fled.'

'Oh, really?' said Loris-Melikov. 'I thought you were never afraid of anything.'

'Afterwards never; since then I have always recalled that shame, and when I recall it, I no longer fear anything.'

12

'But that is enough for now. I need to pray,' said Hadji Murat, then took out from the inner breast pocket of his Circassian coat Vorontsov's Breguet, pressed the mainspring carefully and, inclining his head to one side and restraining his childlike smile, he listened. The watch struck twelve and one quarter.

'My friend Vorontsov's present,' he said, with a smile. 'He is a good man.'

'Yes, he is,' said Loris-Melikov. 'And it's a good watch. So you pray, and I'll wait.'

'*Yakshi*, alright,' said Hadji Murat, and he went off into the bedroom.

Left on his own, Loris-Melikov wrote down in his notebook the main points of what Hadji Murat had told him, then he lit a cigarette and began to walk to and fro around the room. When he went up to the door opposite the bedroom, Loris Melikov heard the animated voices of men speaking about something rapidly in Tatar. He guessed that it was Hadji Murat's followers and, opening the door, he went in to them.

The room was filled with that particular sour smell of leather that mountaineers have. On a cloak on the floor by the window sat one-eyed, red-haired Gamzalo in a ragged, soiled quilted coat, knotting a bridle. He was saying something heatedly in his hoarse voice, but immediately fell silent at Loris-Melikov's entrance and, paying no attention to him, carried on with what he was doing. Opposite him stood cheerful Khan Magoma, who, with white teeth bared, and black, lashless eyes flashing, kept repeating one and the same thing. Handsome Eldar, with sleeves rolled up on his powerful arms, was rubbing at the girths of a saddle that was hanging from a nail. Khanefi, the chief worker who was in charge of the household, was not in the room. He was cooking dinner in the kitchen.

'What was it you were arguing about?' Loris-Melikov asked Khan Magoma after greeting him.

'He keeps on praising Shamil,' said Khan Magoma, giving Loris his hand. 'He says Shamil is a great man. Learned, and holy, and a horseman.'

'How is it that he left him, but still praises him?'

'Left him, but praises him,' pronounced Khan Magoma, teeth bared and eyes shining.

'Well then, and you consider him holy?' asked Loris-Melikov.

'If he were not holy, the people would pay no heed to him,' said Gamzalo quickly.

'It was not Shamil that was holy, but Mansur[17],' said Khan Magoma. 'He was truly holy. When he was imam, all the people were quite different. He would go round the villages, and the people would go out to him, they kissed the skirts of his coat and repented of their sins and swore to do no wrong. The old men used to say that all the people lived like holy men then – not smoking, not drinking, not missing prayers, forgiving one another their grievances, even forgiving blood. At that time, when money and lost articles were found, they were tied to poles and set up on the roads. Then God too gave the people success in everything, not like the way it is now,' said Khan Magoma.

'Even now in the mountains people do not drink and do not smoke,' said Gamzalo.

'Your Shamil is a *lamoroy*,' said Khan Magoma, winking at Loris-Melikov.

Lamoroy was a term of contempt for the mountaineers.

'The *lamoroy* is a mountaineer. Eagles live in the mountains too,' replied Gamzalo.

'Good man! Cut me down neatly,' said Khan Magoma, baring his teeth, pleased at his adversary's neat reply.

Seeing the silver cigarette-case in Loris-Melikov's hand, he asked for something to smoke. And when Loris-Melikov said that they were forbidden to smoke, he winked with his one eye, jerking his head towards Hadji Murat's bedroom, and said that you could smoke when nobody saw you. And he began smoking straight away, not inhaling, and putting his red lips together awkwardly when exhaling the smoke.

'This is not good,' said Gamzalo sternly, and left the room. Khan Magoma winked in his direction too and, while he smoked, he began to question Loris-Melikov about where best to buy a silk quilted coat and a white sheepskin hat.

'What, do you have so much money then?'

'Yes, enough,' said Khan Magoma, with a wink.

'You ask him where his money comes from,' said Eldar, turning his handsome smiling head towards Loris.

'I won it,' began Khan Magoma quickly, and told how the day before, while walking around Tiflis, he came across a crowd of people, Russian batmen and Armenians, playing pitch-and-toss. There was a big kitty: three gold coins and a lot of silver. Khan Magoma immediately understood the way the game was played and, jangling the copper that he had in his pocket, he entered the circle and said that he would play for the lot.

'What do you mean, the lot? Did you have the money?' asked Loris-Melikov.

'I had just twelve kopeks,' said Khan Magoma, baring his teeth.

'But what if you'd lost?'

'There's this.'

And Khan Magoma indicated his pistol.

'What, would you have handed it over?'

'Why hand it over? I would have run off, and if anyone had stopped me, I would have killed them. And that's that.'

Loris-Melikov understood Khan Magoma and Eldar perfectly. Khan Magoma was a convivial fellow, a fast liver, who did not know what to do with his excess energy; always cheerful, frivolous, he played with his own and other people's lives. Because of this playing with life he had come over now to the Russians, and in exactly the same way, because of this playing, was capable of defecting back to Shamil once again tomorrow. Eldar too was perfectly comprehensible: he was a man entirely devoted to his master, placid, strong and firm. For Loris-Melikov only red-haired Gamzalo was incomprehensible. Loris-Melikov could see that this man was not only devoted to Shamil, but felt an insuperable revulsion, contempt, disgust and hatred for all Russians; and for that reason Loris-Melikov could not understand why he had surrendered to the Russians. An idea occurred to Loris-Melikov that was shared by several superior officers too, that Hadji Murat's surrender and his stories of animosity with Shamil were a deception, that he had come over only to spy out the Russians' weak points and, after fleeing back to the mountains, to direct forces to where the Russians were weak. And Gamzalo supported this supposition with the whole of his being. 'Those ones and Hadji Murat himself,' thought Loris-Melikov, 'can conceal their intentions, but this one gives himself away with his unconcealed hatred.'

Loris-Melikov tried to speak with him. He asked him whether he was bored here. But without stopping what he was doing, and squinting with his one eye at Loris-Melikov, he growled hoarsely and abruptly:

'No, I'm not bored.'

And he replied in the same way to all other questions.

While Loris-Melikov was in the servants' room, Hadji Murat's fourth follower came in too, the Avar Khanefi, with a hairy face and neck and a jutting chest, shaggy as if covered in fur. This was a hefty, unthinking workman, always absorbed in his task, who obeyed his master, like Eldar too, unthinkingly.

When he came into the servants' room for rice, Loris-Melikov stopped him and asked where he was from and whether he had been with Hadji Murat for long.

'Five years,' replied Khanefi to Loris-Melikov's question. 'We are from the same village. My father killed his uncle and they wanted to kill me,' he said, calmly gazing into Loris-Melikov's face from beneath his linked eyebrows. 'Then I asked him to accept me as a brother.'

'What does "accept me as a brother" mean?'

'I didn't shave my head or cut my nails for two months, and then I went to them. They let me in to see Patimat, his mother. Patimat gave me her breast and I became his brother.'

Hadji Murat's voice could be heard in the neighbouring room. Eldar immediately recognised the call of his master and, after wiping his hands, he went hurriedly with broad strides into the drawing-room.

'He is summoning you,' he said, coming back.

And, after giving another cigarette to cheerful Khan Magoma, Loris-Melikov went into the drawing-room.

13

When Loris-Melikov entered the drawing-room, Hadji Murat met him with a cheerful face.

'Well then, shall we continue?' he said, settling down on the ottoman.

'Yes, certainly,' said Loris-Melikov. 'I've been in to see your servants, had a talk with them. One of them's a cheerful fellow,' added Loris-Melikov.

'Yes, Khan Magoma is an easy person,' said Hadji Murat.

'And I liked the young, handsome one.'

'Ah, Eldar. He is young, but hard, like iron.'

Both paused.

'So shall I carry on?'

'Yes, do.'

'I told you how the khans were killed. Well, they were killed and Gamzat entered Khunzakh and settled in the palace of the khans,' began Hadji Murat. 'There remained the khans' mother. Gamzat summoned her. She began to reprimand him. He gave a wink to his follower Aselder, and he struck her from behind and killed her.'

'But why did he kill her?' asked Loris-Melikov.

'What else could he do: where the forelegs have crossed, so too must the hind legs. The whole breed needed to be finished off. That is what was done. Shamil killed the youngest, threw him from a cliff. The whole of Avaria submitted to Gamzat, only my brother and I did not want to submit. We needed his blood in return for the khans. We pretended to submit, but thought only of how to take blood from him. We consulted our grandfather and decided to wait until he left the palace and kill him in an ambush. Somebody overheard us and told Gamzat, and he summoned our grandfather and said: "Watch out, if it is true that your grandsons are planning something bad against me, you and they will hang from the same beam. I am doing God's work and I must not be hindered. Go, and remember what I have said." Grandfather came home and told us. Then we decided not to wait, but to do the deed on the first day of the festival in the mosque. Our comrades refused; there remained my brother and I. We took two pistols each, put on cloaks and went to the mosque. Gamzat came in with thirty followers. All of them held drawn sabres. Alongside Gamzat walked Aselder, his favourite follower, the same one that had cut off the head of the khans' mother. When he saw us he called to us to take off our cloaks, and he came up to me. A dagger was in my hand, and I killed him and rushed towards Gamzat. But my brother Osman had already shot at him. Gamzat was still alive and rushed at my brother with his dagger, but I struck the final blow to his head. There were thirty of them, two of us. They killed my brother Osman, but I fought them off, jumped out of a window and got away. When it was learned that Gamzat was dead, all the people rose up and his followers fled, while those who did not flee were all slaughtered.'

Hadji Murat stopped and took a deep breath.

'That was all good,' he continued, 'then everything was spoilt. Shamil took Gamzat's place. He sent envoys to me to say that I should join him against the Russians; but he threatened that if I refused he would sack Khunzakh and kill me. I said I would not join him and would not let him near me.'

'Why was it you didn't join him?' asked Loris-Melikov.

Hadji Murat frowned and did not reply straight away.

'It was not possible. The blood of both my brother Osman and Abununtsal Khan was on Shamil. I did not join him. General Rozen sent me a commission and asked me to be the ruler of Avaria. Everything would have been fine, but Rozen set over Avaria first the Kazikumyk khan Mahomet Mirza, and then Akhmet Khan. The latter came to hate me. He tried to arrange a match between his son and the khans' sister, Saltanet. She was not given to him, and he thought I was to blame for this. He came to hate me and secretly sent his servants to kill me, but I escaped them. Then he slandered me before General Klugenau, saying that I ordered the Avars not to give firewood to the soldiers. He also told him that I had put on a turban – this one,' said Hadji Murat, indicating the turban on his sheepskin hat – 'and that this meant I had gone over to Shamil. The general did not believe it and ordered that I should not be touched. But when the general left for Tiflis, Akhmet Khan did things his own way: with a detachment of soldiers he seized me, put me in chains and tied me to a cannon. I was held like that for six days. On the seventh I was untied and led away to Temir-Khan-Shura. I was taken by forty soldiers with loaded rifles. My hands were tied and the order was given to kill me if I tried to escape. I knew this. When we began to get near, in the vicinity of Moksokh, the path was narrow, and to the right was a steep drop of about a hundred metres; I went over to the edge of the slope, away from the soldier to the right. The soldier tried to stop me, but I jumped down the slope and pulled the soldier after me. The soldier fell to his death, but I remained alive. Ribs, head, arms, a leg – I broke them all. I would have crawled off, but I could not. My head span and I fell asleep. I woke up wet, in a pool of blood. A shepherd saw me. He called some people and I was carried down to a village. My ribs and head healed, my leg healed too, only it grew short.'

And Hadji Murat stretched out his crooked leg.

'It serves, that is good enough,' he said. 'People found out and began visiting me. I got better and moved to Tselmes. Again the Avars invited me to rule them,' said Hadji Murat, with calm, confident pride. 'And I consented.'

Hadji Murat stood up quickly and, getting a portfolio out from his saddle-bags, he took from it two yellowed letters and handed them to Loris-Melikov. The letters were from General Klugenau. Loris-Melikov read them. The first letter said:

Ensign Hadji Murat! You served under me, I was pleased with you and thought you a good man. General Akhmet Khan informed me recently that you are a traitor, that you have put on a turban, that you have dealings with Shamil, that you have taught the people to disobey the Russian authorities. I ordered you to be arrested and brought to me – you escaped; I do not know if this is for the better or for the worse, because I do not know whether you are guilty or not. Now listen to me. If your conscience is clear before the Great Tsar, if you are guilty of nothing, come to me. Fear nobody – I am your protector. The khan will do nothing to you; he himself is under my command, so there is nothing for you to fear.

Then Klugenau wrote that he had always kept his word and been just, and again exhorted Hadji Murat to surrender to him.

When Loris-Melikov had finished the first letter, Hadji Murat took out another letter, but, before passing it to Loris-Melikov, he told how he had answered this first letter.

'I wrote to him that I had indeed worn a turban, not for Shamil though, but for the salvation of my soul, that I did not want, and was not able to go over to Shamil, because through him my father, brothers and relatives had been killed, but that I could not surrender to the Russians either, because I had been dishonoured. In Khunzakh, while I was tied up, a scoundrel had *** on me. And I could not surrender to you until this man had been killed. And most important, I was afraid of the deceitful Akhmet Khan. Then the general sent me this letter,' said Hadji Murat, handing Loris-Melikov the other yellowed piece of paper.

You replied to my letter, thank you, – read Loris-Melikov. *You write that you are not afraid to return, yet that the dishonour done you by one* giaour *forbids this; but I assure you that Russian law is just, and you will see with your own eyes the punishment of the one who dared to insult you – I have already ordered that this be investigated. Listen, Hadji Murat. I have the right to be displeased with you, because you do not trust me or my honour, but I forgive you, knowing the mistrustful nature of mountaineers in general. If your conscience is clear, if you really put on the turban only for the salvation of your soul, then you are in the right and you can boldly look the Russian government and me in the eye; and I assure you that the one who dishonoured you will be punished,* your property will be returned, *and you will see and learn what Russian law means. Particularly as the Russians look at everything differently; in their eyes you have not fallen, because some swine dishonoured you. I myself allowed the men of Gimri to wear the turban and look upon their actions appropriately; consequently, I repeat, you have nothing to fear. Come to me with the man that I am sending to you now; he is true to me,* he is not the servant of your enemies, *but the friend of a man who holds the special attention of the government.*

Then Klugenau again tried to persuade Hadji Murat to surrender.

'I did not believe this,' said Hadji Murat, when Loris-Melikov had finished the letter, 'and I did not go to Klugenau. The main thing was that I needed to have revenge upon Akhmet Khan, and that I could not have it through the Russians. At this very time Akhmet Khan surrounded Tselmes and tried to seize or kill me. I had too few men and could not beat him off. And it was at this time that a man sent by Shamil came to me with a letter. He promised to help me to beat off Akhmet Khan and kill him, and he gave me the whole of Avaria to rule. I thought for a long time and went over to Shamil. And so since that time I have been continually fighting the Russians.'

Here Hadji Murat related all his military deeds. There were very many of them, and Loris-Melikov knew them in part. All his marches and raids were striking in their unusual speed of movement and the boldness of their attacks, which were always crowned with success.

'There was never friendship between me and Shamil,' Hadji Murat concluded his story, 'but he feared me and he needed me. Then it happened, however, that I was asked who was to be imam after Shamil. I said that the imam would be the one who had the sharp sabre. Shamil was told this and he wanted to be rid of me. He sent me to Tabasaran. I went and captured a thousand sheep and three hundred horses. But he said that I had done things wrong, he appointed another governor in my place and ordered me to send him all my money. I sent a thousand gold coins. He sent his followers and took my entire estate away from me. He demanded I go to him; I knew he wanted to kill me and I did not go. He sent men to take me. I fought them off and surrendered to Vorontsov. Only I did not bring my family. My mother and my wife and my son are with him. Tell the chief: while my family is there I can do nothing.'

'I'll tell him,' said Loris-Melikov.

'Try to do what you can. What is mine is yours, only help me with the Prince. I am tied, and the end of the rope is in Shamil's hand.'

With these words Hadji Murat ended his story to Loris-Melikov.

14

On the 20th of December Vorontsov wrote the following to the minister of war, Chernyshov. The letter was in French.

I did not write to you with the last post, my dear Prince, as I wished first to decide what we should do with Hadji Murat, and felt not entirely well for two or three days. In my last letter I informed you of Hadji Murat's arrival here: he came to Tiflis on the eighth; on the next day I made his acquaintance, and for some eight or nine days I spoke with him and thought over what he might subsequently be able to do for us, and particularly what we are to do with him now, since he is most concerned about the fate of his family and says with all the signs of complete candour that, while his family is in the hands of Shamil, he is paralysed and has no capacity to be of service to us and prove his gratitude for the warm reception and forgiveness he has been shown. The ignorance in which he finds himself with regard to persons dear to him arouses in him a feverish state, and those I have appointed to stay with him here assure me that he does not sleep at night, eats almost nothing, prays continually, and asks permission only to go horse-riding with a few Cossacks – the only possible entertainment for him and an essential exercise in consequence of the habit of many years. He has come to see me every day to learn whether I have any news of his family, and he requests that I order the collection on our various lines of all the prisoners who are at our disposal in order to offer them to Shamil in an exchange, to which he will add some money. There are those who will give him money for this purpose. He has repeated to me constantly: 'Save my family, and then give me the opportunity to be of service to you' (best of all, in his opinion, on the Lezghian line) 'and if after a month I have not rendered you a great service, punish me as you consider necessary.'

I replied to him that all this seems to me extremely fair and that many could be found among us who would not trust him if his family stayed in the mountains, and not with us as security; that I would do everything possible for the collection of prisoners on our borders and that, although I did not have the right in accordance with our regulations to give him money for a ransom in addition to what he found himself, I might be able to find other means to help him. After this I told him candidly my opinion that Shamil would on no account hand over his family, that he might perhaps announce this to him directly, promise him complete forgiveness and his former positions, threaten, if he did not return, to destroy his mother, wife and six children. I asked him if he could say frankly what he would do if he received such an announcement from Shamil. Hadji Murat raised his eyes and his arms to the sky and told me that everything is in God's hands, but that he would never give himself up into the hands of his enemy because he was absolutely certain that Shamil would not forgive him and that he would not then remain alive for long. As regards the extermination of his family, he does not think that Shamil will act so foolishly: firstly, so as not to make a still more desperate and dangerous enemy of him; and secondly, there is a host of really very influential figures in Dagestan who would dissuade him from this. Finally he repeated to me several times that whatever might be God's will for the future, he was now occupied only with the idea of ransoming his family; that he implored me in the name of God to help him and allow him to return to the environs of Chechnya, where, through the mediation and with the permission of our commanders, he might have some communication with his family, regular news of their present situation and of ways of liberating them; that many people and even some Tatar governors in this part of the enemy country were more or less attached to him; that in this entire population, already subjugated by the Russians or neutral, it would be a simple matter for him, with our help, to have communications, very useful for the attainment of the goal that tormented him day and night, the fulfilment of which would reassure him so, and would afford him the opportunity to act for our benefit and to earn our trust. He requests me to send him back to Grozny with an escort of twenty or thirty courageous Cossacks who could serve him as a shield from his enemies and us as a guarantee of the truth of his professed intentions.

You will appreciate, my dear Prince, that all this has troubled me a good deal, for, whatever is done, a great responsibility lies on me. It would be incautious in the highest degree to trust him completely; but if we wanted to deprive him of the means to escape, then we would have to lock him up; yet that, in my opinion, would be both unjust and impolitic. Such a measure – word of which would quickly spread through the whole of Dagestan – would do us great harm there, taking away the inclination of all (and there are many) who are prepared to go more or less openly against Shamil and who take such an interest in the position among us of the bravest and most enterprising aide of the imam, who considered himself forced to surrender into our hands. Once we had treated Hadji Murat like a prisoner, the whole positive effect of his betrayal of Shamil would be lost for us.

And so I do not think that I could have acted in any other way than I have, while conscious, however, that it will be possible to accuse me of a great mistake, should it occur to Hadji Murat to leave again. In service and in such tangled affairs it is difficult, not to say impossible, to go down one straight path, without risking error and without taking responsibility upon oneself; but once the path seems straight, one must go down it, come what may.

I beg you, my dear Prince, to submit this for the consideration of His Majesty the Emperor, and I shall be happy if our Most August Sovereign should deign to approve my action. All that I have written to you above I have also written to Generals Zavadovsky and Kozlovsky so that Kozlovsky can communicate directly with Hadji Murat, whom I have warned to do nothing and go nowhere without the approval of the former. I have told him that it is even better for us if he goes out with our escort, otherwise Shamil will start to spread the word that we are holding Hadji Murat under lock and key; but at the same time I have had him promise that he will never go to Vozdvizhenskaya, since my son, to whom he first surrendered himself and whom he considers his kunak (friend), is not the commander of the place, and misunderstandings could occur. Moreover Vozdvizhenskaya is too close to a large hostile population, while for the communications that he wishes to have with his confidants, Grozny is convenient in all respects.

Besides the twenty hand-picked Cossacks who, at his request, will not move a step away from him, I have sent Captain Loris-Melikov, a worthy, excellent and very intelligent officer who speaks Tatar and who knows Hadji Murat well; Hadji Murat appears to trust him absolutely too. For the ten days that Hadji Murat has spent here, incidentally, he has lived in the same house as Lieutenant-Colonel Prince Tarkhanov, commander of the Shushin District, who has been here on matters of service; he is a truly worthy man and I trust him absolutely. He has also earned the trust of Hadji Murat, and through him alone, since he has an excellent command of Tatar, did we discuss the most delicate and secret matters.

I have consulted Tarkhanov about Hadji Murat, and he is entirely in agreement with me that either we had to act as I have acted, or put Hadji Murat in prison and guard him with the strictest possible measures – because once he is treated badly he will be difficult to hold – or else move him out of the country completely. But these two latter measures would not only have nullified all the advantage we have gained from the quarrel between Hadji Murat and Shamil, but would have inevitably stalled any development of disquiet and the possibility of revolt against Shamil's rule among the mountaineers. Prince Tarkhanov told me that he is himself certain of Hadji Murat's sincerity and that Hadji Murat does not doubt that Shamil will never forgive him and will have him executed, in spite of the promised forgiveness. The one thing that has managed to worry Tarkhanov in his relations with Hadji Murat is his attachment to his religion, and he does not conceal the fact that Shamil will be able to influence him from that point of view. But as I have already said above, he will never convince Hadji Murat that he will not take his life, either straight away, or at some time after his return.

That is all, my dear Prince, that I wished to tell you about this episode in affairs here.

15

This report was dispatched from Tiflis on the 24th of December. And on the eve of the New Year of 1852 a courier who had exhausted a dozen horses and beaten a dozen drivers until they bled, delivered it to Prince Chernyshov, the then minister of war.

And on the 1st of January 1852 Chernyshov took to the Emperor Nikolai, among other files, this report of Vorontsov's.

Chernyshov disliked Vorontsov, both for the universal respect that Vorontsov enjoyed, and for his enormous wealth, and for the fact that Vorontsov was a true aristocrat, while Chernyshov was after all a parvenu, and, most important, for the Emperor's particularly good disposition towards Vorontsov. And for that reason Chernyshov exploited every opportunity, so far as he could, to harm Vorontsov. In his last report on affairs in the Caucasus Chernyshov had succeeded in arousing the Emperor's displeasure with Vorontsov over the fact that the carelessness of the authorities had resulted in a small Caucasian detachment being completely wiped out by mountaineers. Now he intended to present Vorontsov's arrangements for Hadji Murat in a disadvantageous light. He wanted to suggest to the sovereign that Vorontsov, who was always offering protection and even indulgence to the natives, to the actual detriment of the Russians, had, in leaving Hadji Murat in the Caucasus, acted unwisely; that in all probability Hadji Murat had surrendered to us only in order to spy on our means of defence, and that for this reason it would be better to dispatch Hadji Murat into the Russian heartland and make use of him only when his family had been rescued from the mountains and it was possible to be assured of his loyalty.

But Chernyshov was unsuccessful with this plan simply because on this morning of the 1st of January Nikolai was particularly out of sorts and just to be contradictory would not have accepted any proposal from anybody; still less was he inclined to accept a proposal from Chernyshov whom he merely suffered, considering him irreplaceable for the moment, but whom, knowing his efforts to destroy Zakhar Chernyshov in the trial of the Decembrists[18], and his attempt to seize Zakhar's fortune, he considered an utter scoundrel. So thanks to Nikolai's bad frame of mind, Hadji Murat remained in the Caucasus and his fate did not change as it might have changed, had Chernyshov made his report at another time.

It was half past nine when, in the mist of a twenty-degree frost, Chernyshov's fat, bearded coachman, in an azure velvet hat with pointed ends, sitting on the box of a small sledge, just like the one in which Nikolai Pavlovich rode, drove up to the small porch of the Winter Palace and gave an affable nod to his friend, Prince Dolgoruky's coachman, who, after helping his master down, had long been waiting by the palace porch with the reins underneath his fat, padded backside, rubbing his frozen hands.

Chernyshov was wearing his uniform, a greatcoat with a fluffy, grey, beaver collar and a tricorn hat with cockerel feathers. Throwing back the bearskin travelling rug, he carefully freed his frozen feet, without overshoes (he took pride in not recognising overshoes), from the sledge, and, trying to feel cheerful, with his spurs ringing, he went over the carpet into the door that a doorman respectfully opened before him. In the entrance hall, throwing his greatcoat off into the arms of an aged footman who came running up to him, Chernyshov went over to a mirror and carefully removed his hat from his curled wig. After looking at himself in the mirror, with an accustomed movement of his old man's hands he pushed up the curls at his temples and on the top of his wig and straightened his cross, aiguillettes and large monogrammed epaulettes, then, stepping weakly on his old man's legs that were slow to obey, he began to ascend the carpeted rising staircase.

Passing the footmen who stood by the doors in dress uniform and bowed to him obsequiously, Chernyshov went into the reception room. The duty officer, a newly appointed aide-de-camp, greeted him respectfully, radiant in his new full dress uniform, epaulettes and aiguillettes, and with his rosy face not yet haggard, but shining, with its black moustache and hair brushed down on the temples towards the eyes, just as Nikolai Pavlovich brushed his. Prince Vasily Dolgoruky, a deputy minister of war, with a bored expression on his slow-witted face, which was adorned with sideburns, moustache and hair on the temples, just the same as Nikolai wore, got up to meet Chernyshov and exchanged greetings with him.

'*L'empereur?*'[19] Chernyshov asked the aide-de-camp, indicating the door of the study with questioning eyes.

'*Sa Majesté est vient de rentrer,*'[20] said the aide-de-camp, listening to the sound of his own voice with evident pleasure, and, stepping gently, so smoothly that a full glass of water placed on his head would not have spilt, he went up to the door, which opened without a sound, and, manifesting with his entire being his respect for the place into which he was stepping, he disappeared behind the door.

Dolgoruky, meanwhile, opened his portfolio, checking the documents it contained.

And Chernyshov walked about with a frown, stretching his legs and trying to remember all that he had to report to the Emperor. Chernyshov was beside the door of the study when it opened again and from it there emerged the aide-de-camp, even more radiant and respectful than before, who with a gesture invited the minister and his deputy in to the sovereign.

The Winter Palace had already long been rebuilt after the fire, but Nikolai still lived on its top floor. The study in which he received high-ranking officials and ministers with reports was a very high-ceilinged room with four large windows. A large portrait of the Emperor Alexander I hung on the main wall. Between the windows stood two bureaux. Along the walls stood several chairs, in the middle of the room a huge writing-desk and in front of the desk Nikolai's armchair and chairs for those he was receiving.

Nikolai, wearing a black frock-coat without epaulettes but with small shoulder-straps, was sitting by the desk with his huge body thrown back and his bulging stomach drawn tightly in, motionlessly watching with his lifeless gaze the men coming in. His long white face with the huge receding forehead jutting out from the smoothed-down hair on his temples, artfully joined to the wig that covered his bald patch, was today particularly cold and motionless. His eyes, always dull, gazed more dully than usual, his pursed lips beneath his upwardly curled moustache, his fattened cheeks, propped up by his high collar, freshly shaven with their neat sausages of sideburns remaining, and his chin, squeezed into his collar, all lent his face an expression of displeasure and even anger. The cause of this mood was tiredness. And the cause of the tiredness was the fact that he had been to a masquerade the night before and, while walking about as usual in his horse-guard's helmet with a bird on it among the public, who crowded towards him yet shyly retreated before his huge and self-confident figure, he met once again the masquer who, at the previous masquerade, having aroused in him an old man's sensuality with her whiteness, beautiful figure and tender voice, had left him with a promise to meet him at the next masquerade. At the previous day's masquerade she had come up to him, and after that he did not let her go. He led her into the box that was held ready especially for this purpose, where he could remain alone with his lady. Reaching the door of the box in silence, Nikolai glanced around, looking out for the box-keeper, but he was not there. Nikolai frowned and pushed the door of the box himself, letting his lady through before him.

'*Il y a quelqu'un*,'[21] said the masquer, stopping. The box was indeed occupied. Close to one another on a velvet couch sat an officer of the lancers and a pretty young woman with blonde curls in a domino with her mask removed. On seeing the angry figure of Nikolai, drawn up to its full height, the blonde woman hurriedly covered her face with her mask, while the uhlan officer, without rising from the couch, rooted to the spot in terror, gazed at Nikolai with motionless eyes.

No matter how accustomed Nikolai was to the terror he aroused in people, he always found this terror pleasing, and he sometimes liked to amaze people who were terror-stricken with the contrast of the affectionate words addressed to them. And that was how he acted now.

'Well, my good fellow, you're a little younger than me,' he said to the officer, who was numb from terror, 'you can let me have your seat.'

The officer leapt up and, in utter confusion, he followed the masquer out of the box, bent double and in silence, and Nikolai was left alone with his lady.

The masquer turned out to be a pretty, innocent girl of twenty, the daughter of a Swedish governess. This girl told Nikolai how even as a child she had fallen in love with him from portraits, had worshipped him and decided to win his attention at any cost. And now she had won it, and, as she said, she needed nothing more. This girl was taken away to the site of Nikolai's customary rendezvous with women, and Nikolai spent more than an hour with her.

When in the night he returned to his room and lay down on the narrow, hard bed of which he was so proud, and covered himself with his cape, which he considered (and he said as much) just as renowned as Napoleon's hat, he could not get to sleep for a long time. He recalled first the frightened and enraptured expression on the white face of this girl, then the statuesque, plump shoulders of his permanent mistress Nelidova, and drew comparisons between the one and the other. That the debauchery of a married man was a bad thing did not even occur to him, and he would have been very surprised if anybody had condemned him for it. But despite the fact that he was certain he had behaved as he should, a certain unpleasant aftertaste remained with him and, in order to stifle this feeling, he began thinking about the thing that always reassured him: about what a great man he was.

Despite the fact that he was late going to sleep, he got up as always before eight o'clock and, when he had completed his customary toilet, rubbing his large, well-fed body with ice, and had prayed to God, saying the usual prayers that he had recited since childhood, 'Mother of God', 'I believe' and 'Our Father', without attaching any significance to the words he was saying, he then went out of the small porch onto the embankment wearing a greatcoat and cap.

In the middle of the embankment he came upon a pupil of the College of Jurisprudence of just such huge height as he was himself, wearing full dress uniform and a hat. Seeing the uniform of the college, which he disliked for its freethinking, Nikolai Pavlovich frowned, but the pupil's great height, assiduous pose at the attention, and his salute with elbow emphatically stuck out mollified his displeasure.

'Your name?' he asked.

'Polosatov, Your Imperial Majesty!'

'Good lad!'

The pupil continued to stand with his hand to his hat. Nikolai stopped.

'Do you want to join the army?'

'No, Your Imperial Majesty.'

'Blockhead!' And Nikolai, turning away, carried on his way and began loudly pronouncing the first words that occurred to him. 'Kopervein, Kopervein,' he repeated the name of the girl from the previous day several times. 'Squalid, squalid.' He did not think about what he was saying, but stifled his feelings by the attention he paid to his utterances. 'Yes, what would Russia be without me,' he said to himself when he sensed once again the approach of a feeling of discontent. 'Yes, what would it be without me, not Russia alone, but Europe.' And he remembered his brother-in-law, the King of Prussia, and his weakness and stupidity, and he shook his head.

Going back towards the porch, he saw Yelena Pavlovna's carriage[22], which with its red-liveried footman was drawing up to the Saltykov entrance. Yelena Pavlovna was for him the embodiment of those empty people who discussed not only the sciences and poetry, but also the government of men, imagining that they could govern themselves better than he, Nikolai, governed them. He knew that, no matter how he pushed these people down, they came to the surface again and again. And he remembered his recently deceased brother, Mikhail Pavlovich. And a feeling of annoyance and sadness gripped him. He frowned gloomily and again began whispering the first words that occurred to him. He stopped whispering only when he entered the palace. He went into his room and, after smoothing down in front of the mirror his sideburns, the hair on his temples and the hairpiece on his crown, and having curled his moustache, he went straight into the study where reports were received.

He received Chernyshov first. From Nikolai's face and, most important, his eyes, Chernyshov immediately realised that he was in a particularly bad mood today, and, knowing of his adventure on the previous day, he realised what was the cause of it. Having greeted Chernyshov coldly and asked him to sit down, Nikolai stared at him with his lifeless eyes.

First of all in Chernyshov's report came the matter of the thieving that had been discovered among commissariat officials, then came the matter of the movement of troops on the Prussian border, then the award of New Year's honours to certain people who had been omitted in the first list; then came Vorontsov's dispatch about Hadji Murat surrendering, and, finally, the unpleasant matter of the student at the Medical Academy who had made an attempt on the life of a professor.

With his lips tightly compressed in silence and his large white hands with one gold ring on the third finger stroking the sheets of paper, Nikolai listened to the report on the thieving without lowering his eyes from Chernyshov's forehead and quiff.

Nikolai was certain that everybody thieved. He knew that now it would be necessary to punish the commissariat officials, and decided to send them all off to the army, but he also knew that this would not prevent those who replaced the dismissed men from doing the same. The nature of officials was that they stole, and it was his duty to punish them and, no matter how tired he might be of it, he conscientiously carried out this duty.

'Here in Russia we evidently have only one honest man,' he said.

Chernyshov immediately realised that this solitary honest man in Russia was Nikolai himself and smiled in agreement.

'It is probably so, Your Majesty,' he said.

'Leave it, I'll put instructions on,' said Nikolai, taking the paper and moving it to the left-hand side of the desk.

After this, Chernyshov began making his reports about the honours and the movement of troops. Nikolai looked through the list, crossed out several names, and then gave brief and decisive instructions for the transfer of two divisions to the Prussian border.

Nikolai could not possibly forgive the Prussian King for the constitution he had granted after 1848, and so, while expressing to his brother-in-law the most friendly sentiments in letters and orally, he considered it necessary to have troops on the Prussian border just in case. These troops might also be needed so that, in the case of revolt among the people in Prussia (Nikolai saw a readiness to revolt everywhere), they could be moved forward in defence of his brother-in-law's throne, as he had moved troops forward in the defence of Austria against the Hungarians. These troops were also needed on the border in order to lend greater weight and significance to his advice to the Prussian King.

'Yes, what would be happening to Russia now, were it not for me,' he thought again.

'Well, what else?' he said

'A courier from the Caucasus,' said Chernyshov, and began to report what Vorontsov had written about Hadji Murat surrendering.

'You don't say!' said Nikolai. 'A good start.'

'Evidently the plan devised by Your Majesty is beginning to bear fruit,' said Chernyshov.

This praise of his strategic capabilities was especially pleasing to Nikolai, for although he took pride in his strategic capabilities, deep down in his heart he was conscious that he had none. And now he wanted to hear himself praised in greater detail.

'How do you see it?'

'The way I see it is that if we had long been following Your Majesty's plan, gradually, albeit slowly moving forward, cutting down the forests, destroying reserves, then the Caucasus would have been subdued long ago. I put Hadji Murat's surrender down to this alone. He realises that they can hold out no longer.'

'That's right,' said Nikolai.

Despite the fact that the plan for slow movement into enemy territory by means of the felling of forests and the destruction of provisions was the plan of Yermolov and Velyaminov, and the complete opposite of Nikolai's plan, whereby it was necessary to seize Shamil's residence at once and sack that nest of brigands, and whereby the Dargo expedition of 1845 had been undertaken, costing the lives of so many men – despite this, Nikolai ascribed the plan for slow movement, the systematic felling of forests and the destruction of provisions to himself as well. It would have seemed that in order to believe that the plan for slow movement, the felling of forests and the destruction of provisions was his plan, it was necessary to conceal the fact that he had absolutely insisted on the completely contradictory military undertaking of 1845. But he did not conceal this, and was proud both of that plan for his expedition of 1845, and of the plan for slow movement forward, despite the fact that these two plans were clearly contradictory to one another. The constant, clear, vile blatancy of the flattery of those around him had brought him to the point where he no longer saw his contradictions, no longer adapted his actions and words to reality, to logic, or even to simple good sense, but was absolutely certain that all his instructions, no matter how senseless, unjust and mutually incompatible, became entirely sensible, just and mutually compatible simply because it was he that gave them.

And such was his decision concerning the student of the Medical and Surgical Academy, about whom Chernyshov began to report after his report on the Caucasus.

The affair consisted in the fact that the young man, who had failed an examination twice, took it a third time, and when once again the examiner would not pass him, the neurotic student, seeing in this an injustice, seized a penknife from the desk and attacked the professor in some sort of frenzied fit, inflicting on him a number of insignificant wounds.

'What's his name?' asked Nikolai.

'Brzezowski.'

'A Pole?'

'Of Polish descent and a Catholic,' replied Chernyshov.

Nikolai frowned.

He had done a lot of harm to the Poles. To explain this harm he had to be certain that all Poles were scoundrels. And Nikolai considered them such, and hated them in proportion to the harm he had done them.

'Wait a little,' he said and, closing his eyes, he lowered his head.

Chernyshov knew, having heard this a number of times from Nikolai, that when he needed to decide some important question, he had only to concentrate for a few moments, and that then inspiration came upon him and the best possible decision formed all by itself, as if some inner voice were telling him what should be done. He thought now about how he could satisfy most fully that feeling of malice towards the Poles which had been stirred within him by the story of this student, and his inner voice suggested to him the following decision. He took the report and wrote in the margin in his large hand: '*Deserves capital punishment. But, thank God, we have no capital punishment. And it is not for me to introduce it. Let him run the gauntlet of a thousand men twelve times. Nikolai.*' And he signed it with his unnatural, huge flourish.

Nikolai knew that being struck twelve thousand times with rods was not only certain, agonising death, but excessive cruelty, as five thousand blows sufficed to kill the strongest man. But he found it pleasant to be implacably cruel, and pleasant to think that Russia had no capital punishment.

When he had written his resolution concerning the student, he pushed it over to Chernyshov.

'There,' he said. 'Read it.'

Chernyshov read it, and as a sign of reverential surprise at the wisdom of the decision, he bent his head.

'And send all the students out onto the parade ground to be present at the punishment,' added Nikolai.

'It'll be good for them. I'll stamp out this spirit of revolution, I'll tear it out by the roots,' he thought.

'Yes, sir,' said Chernyshov and, after a short silence, having adjusted his quiff, he returned to the report on the Caucasus.

'And how do you order me to write to Mikhail Semyonovich?'

'Adhere firmly to my system of sacking homes and destroying provisions in Chechnya and harrying them with raids,' said Nikolai.

'And what are your orders concerning Hadji Murat?' asked Chernyshov.

'Well, Vorontsov writes that he wants to use him in the Caucasus.'

'Is that not risky?' said Chernyshov, avoiding Nikolai's glance. 'I fear Mikhail Semyonovich is too trusting.'

'And what would you have thought?' Nikolai challenged him sharply, noticing Chernyshov's intention to present Vorontsov's arrangement in a bad light.

'Well, I should have thought it safer to send him to Russia.'

'You thought,' said Nikolai mockingly. 'Well I think not, and am in agreement with Vorontsov. Write that to him.'

'Yes, sir,' said Chernyshov and, getting up, began taking his leave.

Dolgoruky, who during the whole report had said only a few words to Nikolai's questions on the transfer of troops, took his leave too.

After Chernyshov, Nikolai received the governor-general of the Western Region, Bibikov, who had come to take his leave. After expressing approval of the measures taken by Bibikov against the rebellious peasants who had been unwilling to convert to Orthodoxy, he ordered him to try all those remaining recalcitrant in a military court. This meant sentencing them to run the gauntlet. In addition he ordered the newspaper editor who had published information about the transfer of several thousand state peasants to the Crown to be sent to serve in the army as a private.

'I am doing this because I consider it necessary,' he said. 'And I permit no discussion of it.'

Bibikov fully understood the cruelty of the instruction regarding the Uniate Church members and the injustice of the translation of state peasants, who were the only free ones at that time, into crown peasants, that is into serfs of the imperial family. But it was impossible to object. Not to agree with Nikolai's instruction meant losing everything of the brilliant position he had spent forty years acquiring and which he exploited. And for that reason he obediently bent his greying black head as a sign of obedience and readiness to carry out the cruel, senseless and dishonourable imperial will.

After releasing Bibikov, Nikolai, with the consciousness of duty well done, stretched, glanced at the clock, and went to dress to go out. Having put on full dress uniform with epaulettes, decorations and a sash, he went out into the reception halls, where, lined up in their assigned places, more than a hundred men and women in full dress uniform and elegant, low-necked dresses were awaiting his emergence in trepidation.

With lifeless gaze, puffed-out chest and tightly laced stomach, which protruded both above and below the lacing, he went out to those waiting and, sensing that all gazes were turned with timorous servility upon him, he adopted a still more solemn air. When his eyes met with familiar faces, he stopped, trying to remember who was who, said a few words, sometimes in Russian, sometimes in French, and, piercing them with his cold, lifeless gaze, listened to what they said to him.

After accepting their congratulations, Nikolai passed into the chapel.

God greeted and praised Nikolai through His servants, just as the laymen had, and he accepted these greetings and praises as his due, even if he was bored with them. It all had to be this way, because on him depended the prosperity and happiness of the whole world, and although this tired him, nevertheless he did not refuse the world his good offices. When at the end of Mass the magnificent, coiffured deacon proclaimed 'Many Years' and the choristers harmoniously took up these words with their fine voices, Nikolai, looking around, noticed Nelidova with her luxuriant shoulders standing by a window, and decided in her favour the comparison with the girl of the day before.

After Mass he went to see the Empress and spent several minutes in the family circle, joking with the children and his wife. Then he dropped in via the Hermitage on the Minister of the Court Volkonsky and, among other things, ordered him to pay out an annual pension from special funds to the mother of the girl of the day before. And leaving him, he set off on his usual ride.

Dinner on this day was in the Pompeii Hall; invited besides his younger sons, Nikolai and Mikhail, were Baron Lieven, Count Rzhevussky, Dolgoruky, the Prussian envoy and the Prussian king's aide-de-camp.

While they were waiting for the Empress and the Emperor to appear, an interesting conversation was struck up between the Prussian envoy and Baron Lieven regarding the latest alarming news received from Poland.

'*La Pologne et le Caucase, ce sont les deux cautères de la Russie,*' said Lieven. '*Il nous faut cent mille hommes à peu-près dans chaqu'un de ces deux pays.*'[23]

The envoy affected surprise that this was the case.

'*Vous dîtes, la Pologne?*'[24] he said.

'*Oh oui, c'était un coup de maître de Metternich de nous en avoir laissé l'embarras...*'[25]

At this point in the conversation the Empress entered with her shaking head and frozen smile, followed by Nikolai.

At the table Nikolai talked about Hadji Murat surrendering and about the fact that the war in the Caucasus should now soon be at an end as a result of his arrangement to constrain the mountaineers by the felling of forests and a system of fortifications.

The envoy, exchanging a rapid glance with the Prussian aide-de-camp, with whom he had been talking just that morning about Nikolai's unfortunate weakness in considering himself a great strategist, was full of praise for this plan, which proved once again Nikolai's great strategic capabilities.

After dinner Nikolai went to the ballet, where hundreds of naked women marched about in body stockings. He took a fancy to one in particular and, summoning the ballet-master, Nikolai thanked him and ordered him to be presented with a diamond ring.

The next day, during Chernyshov's report, Nikolai confirmed once again his instruction to Vorontsov to intensify the harrying of Chechnya, now that Hadji Murat had surrendered, and to squeeze it within a cordon of forts.

Chernyshov wrote to Vorontsov in these terms and another courier galloped to Tiflis, exhausting horses and punching drivers in the face.

16

Straight away, in January 1852, in execution of this order from Nikolai Pavlovich, a raid was carried out on Chechnya.

The detachment assigned to the raid consisted of four battalions of infantry, two hundred Cossacks and eight guns. The column marched along the road, while on both sides of the column in an unbroken line, going up and down across gullies, went chasseurs in high boots, sheepskin jackets and sheepskin hats, with rifles on their shoulders and cartridges on cross-belts. As always, the detachment moved across hostile ground observing silence as far as possible. Only occasionally did the shaking guns clatter over ditches, or an artillery horse, which did not understand the order for quiet, snort or neigh, or an angry officer shout in a hoarse, restrained voice at his subordinates because the line had become too extended, or was too far from, or too close to the column. Only once was the silence broken when from a thicket of thorns located between the line and the column there sprang a nanny-goat with a white belly and behind and a grey back, and a similar billy-goat with small horns curving onto his back. The beautiful, frightened animals swooped so close to the column in great leaps with their forelegs tucked up, that some of the soldiers, shouting and laughing, ran after them, meaning to bayonet them, but the goats turned back, slipped through the line, and, pursued by a few horsemen and the company dogs, flew off like birds into the mountains.

It was still winter, but the sun was beginning to climb higher, and at midday, when the detachment, having set out in the early morning, had already covered some ten kilometres, it was strong enough for it to become hot, and its rays were so bright that it hurt to look at the steel of the bayonets and the flashes that suddenly flared up like little suns on the bronze of the cannon.

Behind was the fast-flowing, clear little river that the detachment had just crossed, ahead were cultivated fields and meadows with shallow gullies, still further ahead were mysterious black mountains, covered in forest, and beyond the black mountains were cliffs, jutting out still further, and on the high horizon were the ever delightful, ever changing snow-capped mountains, playing in the light like diamonds.

At the head of the Fifth Company, in a black frock-coat and sheep-skin hat and with a sabre over his shoulder, walked a tall, handsome officer named Butler, who had recently transferred from the Guards, experiencing the invigorating feeling of the joy of life and at the same time the danger of death, and the desire for action, and the con-sciousness of belonging to a huge whole, governed by a single will. Butler was today going into action for the second time, and he felt glad at the idea that at any minute he would start to be shot at, and that not only would he not duck his head beneath a cannon-ball flying past or pay no attention to the whistling of bullets, but, as had already been the case with him, would raise his head higher and look around at his fellow officers and soldiers with a smile in his eyes and start to talk about something else in the most indifferent voice.

The detachment turned off the good road and onto one that was little used and went through a field of maize stubble, and was beginning to approach the forest when – it could not be seen from where – a cannon-ball flew by with an ominous whistling and, ploughing up the earth, hit the middle of a string of carts in the maize field alongside the road.

'It's starting,' said Butler, with a cheerful smile to the officer walking next to him.

And indeed, after the cannon-ball there appeared from out of the forest a dense group of mounted Chechens with pennants. In the middle of the group was a large green pennant, and the old company sergeant-major, who was very long-sighted, informed the short-sighted Butler that this must be Shamil himself. The group came down the hill, appeared on the crest of the nearest gully to the right and began to descend. The little general in a warm black frock-coat and sheepskin hat with a big white lambskin rode up to Butler's company on his ambler and ordered him to move to the right against the descending horsemen. Butler quickly led his company in the direction indicated, but had not yet had time to go down towards the gully when he heard from behind him two cannon-shots one after the other. He looked back: two clouds of blue-grey smoke had risen above two cannon and drifted along the gully. The group, who had evidently not been expecting artillery, turned back. Butler's company began firing in the wake of the mountaineers, and the entire depression became shrouded in powder-smoke. Only above the depression could the mountaineers be seen hurriedly retreating and returning fire at the Cossacks pursuing them. The detachment followed on behind the mountaineers, and on the slope of a second gully there appeared a village.

Butler entered the village with his company at the double after the Cossacks. None of the inhabitants was there. The soldiers were ordered to set light to the grain, the hay and the huts themselves. Acrid smoke spread throughout the village, and soldiers darted in and out of this smoke, dragging whatever they found out of the huts, and, most importantly, catching and shooting the hens that the mountaineers had not been able to take away. The officers sat down some distance from the smoke and had lunch and a drink. The sergeant-major brought them some honeycombs on a board. Nothing could be heard of the Chechens. A little after midday the order was given to withdraw. The companies drew up into a column outside the village and Butler was obliged to be in the rearguard. As soon as they moved off, the Chechens appeared and, following the detachment, accompanied it with gunshots.

When the detachment came out into the open the mountaineers fell back. None of Butler's men was wounded, and he was returning in the most cheerful and bright frame of mind.

When, after wading back across the river they had crossed in the morning, the detachment stretched out across the maize fields and meadows, the singers stepped out in front of their companies and songs rang out. There was no wind, the air was fresh, clear and so transparent that the snow-capped mountains a hundred kilometres away seemed very close and when the singers fell quiet, the regular tramp of feet and rattling of cannon could be heard like a background against which each song began and ended. The song that was sung in Butler's Fifth Company had been composed by a cadet to the glory of the regiment and was sung to a dance tune with the chorus: 'How much better, how much better, my chasseurs, my chasseurs!'

Butler was on horseback alongside his immediate superior, Major Petrov, with whom he shared quarters, and could not have been happier with his decision to leave the Guards and go off to the Caucasus. The main reason for his transfer from the Guards was the fact that he had lost heavily at cards in St Petersburg and had nothing left. He was afraid that he would not have the strength to restrain himself from gambling if he stayed in the Guards, and there was no longer anything for him to lose. Now all this was finished. Here was another life, and such a fine and dashing one. Now he had forgotten both his ruin and the debts he could not pay. And the Caucasus, the war, the soldiers, the officers, the drunken and good-natured Major Petrov – all this seemed so good to him that sometimes he could not believe that he was not in St Petersburg, was not bending back the corners of cards and betting in smoky rooms, hating the banker and feeling a crushing pain in his head, but was here in this wonderful country among these dashing men of the Caucasus.

'How much better, how much better, my chasseurs, my chasseurs!' sang his singers. His horse stepped out merrily to this music. Shaggy, grey Trezorka, the company dog, ran at the head of Butler's company as if he were an officer, with his tail curled and a preoccupied look. In his heart Butler was bright, calm and cheerful. War presented itself to him only in the sense that he subjected himself to danger, the possibility of death, and in so doing earned both decorations and the respect both of his comrades here and his friends in Russia. The other side of war – death, the wounds of soldiers, officers, mountaineers – strange as it might be to say it, did not present itself to his imagination. Subconsciously, so as to sustain his poetic conception of war, he never even looked at the dead and wounded. So it had been today – there were three Russians killed and twelve wounded. He passed by a corpse lying on its back, and only saw with one eye the strange sort of position of a waxen hand and the dark red stain on the head, and did not begin to look in detail. The mountaineers presented themselves to him only as skilled horsemen against whom one had to defend oneself.

'So there you are then, old chap,' said the major in a break in the singing. 'Not the way you do things up there in Petersburg: dressing by the right, dressing by the left. But we do a job and then – home. Mashurka will soon be serving us a pie, some nice cabbage soup. What a life! Eh? Come on, "As dawn came up",' he said, ordering his favourite song.

The major lived as man and wife with the daughter of a doctor's assistant, who had been known as Mashka at first, but later on as Maria Dmitriyevna. Maria Dmitriyevna was a pretty blonde, covered in freckles, a thirty-year-old woman with no children. Whatever her past might have been, she was now the faithful helpmeet of the major, she looked after him like a nanny, and this was something the major needed, as he often drank himself into a stupor.

When they arrived at the fortress everything was as the major had foreseen. Maria Dmitriyevna fed him and Butler and two other officers he invited from the detachment with a filling, tasty dinner, and the major ate and drank so much that he could no longer talk and went off to bed. Butler, tired as well, but contented, and having drunk a little too much strong local wine, went to his room and had hardly got undressed before, laying his palm under his handsome curly head, he fell into a deep sleep without dreams or awakenings.

17

The village sacked in the raid was the very one in which Hadji Murat had spent the night before he went over to the Russians.

Sado, with whom Hadji Murat had stayed, was leaving for the mountains with his family as the Russians approached the village. On returning to his village, Sado found his hut ruined: the roof had fallen in, the door and the pillars of the gallery had been burnt, and the interior had been defiled. His son, the handsome boy with the shining eyes who had looked at Hadji Murat in rapture, was carried dead to the mosque on a horse covered with a felt cloak. He had been bayoneted in the back. The fine-looking woman who had served Hadji Murat during his visit now stood over her son with her shirt ripped at the chest, revealing her old, pendulous breasts, and, with her hair hanging loose, she scratched at her face until it bled, howling incessantly. Sado went off with his relatives carrying a pick and a spade to dig a grave for his son. The old grandfather sat by the wall of the ruined hut and, whittling a stick, gazed dully into space. He had only just returned from his bee-garden. The two small haystacks that were there had been burnt; the apricot and cherry trees that the old man had planted and cared for had been damaged and scorched and, most important, all the beehives had been burnt. Women's howling could be heard in every house and on the square, to which two more bodies had been brought. The small children were bawling along with their mothers. The hungry livestock, for which there was no food, was bawling too. The big children were not playing, but looking at their elders with frightened eyes.

The fountain had been fouled, evidently on purpose, so that water could not be taken from it. Similarly defiled was the mosque, and the mullah and his pupils were cleansing it.

The elders of the village had gathered on the square and, squatting down, were discussing their position. Nobody even spoke of hatred for the Russians. The feeling that all the Chechens, both young and old, experienced was stronger than hatred. It was not hatred, but the refusal to recognise these Russian dogs as people, and such revulsion, disgust and bewilderment before the ridiculous cruelty of these beings, that the desire for their destruction, like the desire for the destruction of rats, poisonous spiders and wolves, was just as natural a feeling as the feeling of self-preservation.

Before the villagers stood a choice: to remain in their homes and restore at dreadful cost in effort everything that had been set up with such labour, and then annihilated so easily and senselessly, waiting for the same thing to be repeated at any moment, or, contrary to religious law and the feeling of revulsion and contempt for the Russians, to submit to them.

The elders prayed and decided unanimously to send envoys to Shamil, asking him for help, and they immediately set about the restoration of what had been damaged.

18

On the second day after the raid, when it was already quite late in the morning, Butler came out from the back porch into the street, intending to take a walk and get a breath of fresh air before his morning tea, which he usually drank together with Petrov. The sun had already come out from behind the mountains, and it hurt to look at the white daub cottages it lit up on the right-hand side of the street, but on the other hand, as always, it was cheering and calming to look to the left at the black mountains that went away and rose up, covered in forests, and at the matt chain of snow-capped mountains, visible from beyond the gorge, that were trying, as always, to pretend to be clouds.

Butler looked at these mountains, drew in lungfuls of air and rejoiced at the fact that he was alive, and that it was precisely he that was alive, and in this beautiful world. He also rejoiced a little at the fact that he had conducted himself so well yesterday in action, both in the advance and, in particular, in the retreat, when the action was quite heated, and he rejoiced at the memory of how yesterday, on returning from the march, Masha, or Maria Dmitriyevna, Petrov's mistress, had entertained them and been particularly informal and nice with everyone, but had been in particular, as it seemed to him, friendly with him. Maria Dmitriyevna, with her thick plait, broad shoulders, high bust and radiant smile on her kind, freckle-covered face, involuntarily attracted Butler as a strong young bachelor, and it even seemed to him that she wanted him. But he considered that this would be wrong in relation to a kind, simple-hearted comrade, and he maintained with Maria Dmitriyevna the most simple, respectful manner, and was pleased with himself for this. He was thinking about this now.

His thoughts were distracted by the frequent clattering that he heard of horses' hooves on the dusty road ahead of him, as though several men were riding at a gallop. He raised his head and saw at the end of the street a crowd of horsemen approaching at walking pace. At the head of a couple of dozen Cossacks rode two men: one in a white Circassian coat and a tall sheepskin hat with a turban, the other an officer in the Russian service, dark, with a hooked nose, in a blue Circassian coat with an abundance of silver on his clothing and weapons. Beneath the rider in the turban was a red-skewbald beauty of a horse with a small head and fine eyes; beneath the officer was a tall, dainty Karabakh horse. Butler, a lover of horses, immediately appreciated the energy and power of the first horse and stopped to find out who these people were. The officer turned to Butler:

'This military commander house?' he asked, betraying both by his ungrammatical speech and his accent his non-Russian origins and indicating with his whip the house of Ivan Matveyevich.

'This very one,' said Butler.

'And who's this then?' asked Butler, moving closer to the officer and indicating with his eyes the man in the turban.

'This Hadji Murat. Come here, will stay here with military commander,' said the officer.

Butler knew about Hadji Murat and about his surrender to the Russians, but did not at all expect to see him here in this small fort.

Hadji Murat looked at him amicably.

'Hello, *koshkoldy*,' he said, using the greeting he had learnt in Tatar.

'*Saubul*,' replied Hadji Murat, nodding his head. He rode up to Butler and offered his hand, on two fingers of which there hung his whip.

'Commander?' he said.

'No, the commander's here, I'll go and call him,' said Butler, addressing the officer as he went up the steps and pushed the door.

But the door of 'the front porch', as Maria Dmitriyevna called it, was locked. Butler knocked, but, receiving no reply, he went round to the back entrance. After calling for his valet and receiving no reply and finding neither of the two valets, he went into the kitchen. Maria Dmitriyevna, all flushed and with a scarf on her head, with her sleeves rolled up above her plump white hands, was cutting up rolled pastry, just as white as her hands were, into small pieces for pies.

'Where have the valets got to?' said Butler.

'They've gone off on a drinking spree,' said Maria Dmitriyevna. 'What is it you want?'

'The door unlocked; you've got a whole horde of mountaineers in front of your house. Hadji Murat's arrived.'

'Tell me another one,' said Maria Dmitriyevna, with a smile.

'I'm not joking. It's true. They're standing by the porch.'

'Not really, surely?' said Maria Dmitriyevna.

'Why should I tell you stories? Go and look, they're standing by the porch.'

'Well, there's a surprise,' said Maria Dmitriyevna, letting down her sleeves and feeling for the pins in her thick plait. 'Well, I'll go and wake Ivan Matveyevich up,' she said.

'No, I'll go myself. And you, Bondarenko, go and unlock the door,' said Butler.

'Well, that'll do too,' said Maria Dmitriyevna, and got on with her work once more.

On learning that Hadji Murat had come to see him, Ivan Matveyevich, who had already heard that Hadji Murat was in Grozny, was not at all surprised, but, sitting up, rolled a cigarette, lit it, and began dressing, coughing loudly and grumbling about his superiors who had sent 'this devil' to him. When he was dressed, he demanded 'some medicine' from his valet. And the valet, knowing that what he called medicine was vodka, served him some.

'There's nothing worse than mixing,' he grumbled, knocking back the vodka and then eating some black bread. 'I drank some local wine yesterday, and I've got a headache. Well, now I'm ready,' he finished, and went into the drawing-room, where Butler had already brought Hadji Murat and the officer accompanying him.

The officer travelling with Hadji Murat handed to Ivan Matveyevich the order from the commander of the left flank to receive Hadji Murat and, while allowing him to have communications with the mountaineers through scouts, on no account to let him out of the fort other than with an escort of Cossacks.

Having read the document, Ivan Matveyevich looked intently for a moment at Hadji Murat and began going through the document again. After transferring his eyes from the document to his guest several times in this way, he finally fixed his eyes on Hadji Murat and said:

'*Yakshi, bek-yakshi*. Let him stay. Tell him that I'm ordered not to let him out. And an order's sacred. And we'll put him – what do you think, Butler? – shall we put him in the office?'

Butler had not had time to reply before Maria Dmitriyevna, who had come from the kitchen and was standing in the doorway, turned to Ivan Matveyevich:

'Why in the office? Put him in here. We'll give him the guest-room and the storeroom. At least you'll keep him in sight,' she said and, glancing at Hadji Murat and meeting his eyes, hurriedly turned away.

'Why, I think Maria Dmitriyevna's right,' said Butler.

'Go on, be off with you, women have no business here,' said Ivan Matveyevich, with a frown.

Throughout the whole conversation Hadji Murat sat with his h.
at the hilt of his dagger and with a slightly contemptuous smile.
said it was all the same to him where he stayed. The one thing that I.
needed and which was permitted him by the chief, was that he should
have communications with the mountaineers, and for that reason he
wished them to be allowed to see him. Ivan Matveyevich said that this
would be done, and asked Butler to entertain the guests until they had
been brought a bite to eat and their rooms had been prepared, while he
himself would go to the office to write out the necessary documents and
make the necessary arrangements.

Hadji Murat's attitude to his new acquaintances was immediately
very clearly defined. From his first meeting with him, Hadji Murat felt
revulsion and contempt towards Ivan Matveyevich, and always treated
him with arrogance. He particularly liked Maria Dmitriyevna, who
cooked and brought him his food. He liked her simplicity, and the
particular beauty of a people alien to him, and the attraction she felt for
him which unconsciously transmitted itself to him. He tried not to look
at her, not to speak to her, but his eyes involuntarily turned towards her
and followed her movements.

And with Butler he immediately became friendly from their very first
meeting, and he willingly talked with him a lot, questioning him about
his life and telling him about his own, and informing him of the news
that was brought to him by scouts about the situation of his family, and
even consulting him about what he was to do.

The news passed on to him by scouts was not good. During the four
days that he spent in the fort they came to him twice, and the news was
bad both times.

19

Soon after he went over to the Russians, Hadji Murat's family was taken
to the village of Vedeno and held there under guard to await Shamil's
decision. The women – old Patimat and Hadji Murat's two wives – and
their five youngest children lived under guard in the hut of the officer
Ibrahim Rashid, while Hadji Murat's son Yusuf, a young man of
eighteen, was in a dungeon, that is in a pit more than two metres deep,
with four criminals, waiting, just like him, for their fate to be decided.

ɔ decision was forthcoming because Shamil was away. He was ɔpaigning against the Russians.

In January 1852 Shamil was returning home to Vedeno after a battle with the Russians in which, in the opinion of the Russians, he had been crushed and made to flee to Vedeno, while in his opinion and the opinion of all his followers, he had won the victory and driven off the Russians. There was a very rare occurrence in this battle, when he himself fired his rifle and, pulling out his sabre, tried to set off on his horse directly towards the Russians, but the followers accompanying him restrained him. Two of them were killed right alongside Shamil.

It was midday when Shamil rode up to his residence, surrounded by a group of his followers showing off their horsemanship around him, firing their rifles and pistols, and incessantly singing '*Lya illyakha il Allah*'.

All the people of the large village of Vedeno were standing in the street and on the roofs to meet their lord, and to mark the triumph they too were firing rifles and pistols. Shamil rode a white Arab horse which trampled gaily on its reins as it came close to home. The horse's harness was extremely plain, without gold or silver decorations: a finely curried red belt bridle with a stripe down the middle, metal cupped stirrups and a red saddle-cloth showing from beneath the saddle. The imam was wearing a fur coat covered with brown cloth, with black fur showing around the neck and the sleeves, strapped onto his long, slender figure with a black dagger-belt. On his head he wore a tall, flat-topped sheepskin hat with a black tassel and a white turban wound around it, the end of which hung down behind his neck. His feet were in green slippers and his calves were wrapped in black leggings, edged with plain laces.

The imam wore nothing shiny, no gold or silver whatsoever, and his tall, erect, powerful figure in clothing without decoration, surrounded by his followers with gold and silver decorations on their clothes and weapons, created that very impression of greatness that he wished, and knew how to create among the people. His pale face, fringed with a trimmed red beard, with its small eyes constantly screwed up, was like stone, utterly immobile. Riding through the village he felt thousands of eyes directed towards him, but his eyes looked at no one. Hadji Murat's wives and children went out onto the gallery too, along with all the inhabitants of the village, to watch the entrance of the imam. Only old Patimat, Hadji Murat's mother, did not go out, but stayed sitting as she had been sitting on the floor of the hut, with tousled greying hair, long arms wrapped around her thin knees, and, blinking her fiery black eyes, looked at the branches burning out in the fireplace. She, just like her son, had always hated Shamil, and did so now even more than before, and she did not want to see him.

Neither did Hadji Murat's son see Shamil's triumphant entrance. He only heard the shooting and singing from his dark and stinking pit and suffered, as only young people, full of life and deprived of freedom, can suffer. Sitting in a stinking pit and constantly seeing the same miserable, dirty, emaciated men he was imprisoned with, who for the most part hated one another, he was now passionately envious of those men who, enjoying air, light and freedom, were now prancing on spirited horses around their lord, shooting and singing in chorus 'Lya illyakha il Allah'.

When he had ridden through the village, Shamil rode into a large courtyard which adjoined an inner one in which was located Shamil's seraglio. Two armed Lezghians met Shamil at the open gates of the first courtyard. This courtyard was full of people. There were men who had come from distant parts on business of their own, there were petitioners, there were those that Shamil had summoned himself for trial and judgement. At Shamil's entrance all those in the courtyard rose and greeted the imam respectfully, putting their hands to their chests. Some knelt down and remained kneeling while Shamil crossed the courtyard from the one set of outer gates to the other, inner ones. Although Shamil recognised among those awaiting him many faces that were unpleasant for him and many dull petitioners demanding to be cared for, he rode past them with the same immutably stony face and, riding into the inner courtyard, dismounted onto the gallery of his quarters, to the left on entering the gates.

After the strain of the campaign, not so much physical as spiritual, because Shamil, despite his public acknowledgement that the campaign had been victorious, knew that the campaign had been unsuccessful, that many Chechen villages had been burnt and sacked and the fickle, frivolous Chechen people were wavering, and some of them, the closest to the Russians, were already prepared to go over to them – this was all difficult, measures needed to be taken against it, but at this moment Shamil did not want to do anything, did not want to think about anything. Now he wanted only two things: rest and the delight of the conjugal caress of the most beloved of his wives, the eighteen-year-old, black-eyed, fleet of foot Kistin girl Aminet.

Yet not only was it impossible even to think of now seeing Aminet, who was right there behind the fence in the inner courtyard that divided the wives' quarters from the men's section (Shamil was certain that even now, while he was dismounting from his horse, Aminet and his other wives were looking through a gap in the fence), and not only was it impossible to go and see her, it was even impossible simply to lie down on the feather beds to recover from his tiredness. First of all it was necessary to carry out the rite of midday prayer, for which he did not now have the least inclination, yet which it was impossible for him not to fulfil in his position as the religious leader of his people, and which was furthermore just as essential for him himself as his daily food. And he carried out his ablutions and prayer. When he had finished praying, he summoned those who had been waiting for him.

First to come in and see him was his father-in-law and teacher, a tall, grey-haired, fine-looking elder with a beard as white as snow and a rosy-red face, Jemal Edin, and, after praying to God, he began questioning Shamil about the events of the campaign, and telling him about what had happened in the mountains during his absence.

Among all sorts of events – revenge killings, cattle theft, accusations of failure to observe the injunctions of the Tarikat, namely the smoking of tobacco and the drinking of wine – Jemal Edin informed him of how Hadji Murat had sent men out to take his family away to the Russians, but that this had been discovered, and the family brought to Vedeno, where they were to be found under guard, awaiting the decision of the imam. In the guest-room next door the elders were gathered for discussion of all these matters, and Jemal Edin advised Shamil to release them that same day, as they had already been waiting for him for three days.

After eating dinner in his room, brought to him by his sharp-nosed, dark, unpleasant to look at, unloved but senior wife Zaidet, Shamil went to the guest-room.

The six men who made up his council, old men with white, grey and red beards, in turbans and without, in tall sheepskin hats and new quilted and Circassian coats, done up with dagger-belts, stood up to greet him. Shamil was a head taller than all of them. Just as he did, they all raised their hands with the palms uppermost and, closing their eyes, said a prayer, then wiped their faces with their hands, running them down their beards and joining them together. When they had finished doing this, they all sat down, with Shamil in the middle on a higher cushion, and discussion began of all the business before them.

The cases of those accused of crimes were decided according to the Sharia: two men were condemned to have their hands chopped off for thieving, one to be beheaded for murder, three were pardoned. Then they set about the main business: the consideration of measures against the defection of Chechens to the Russians. To counteract these defections, Jemal Edin had composed the following proclamation:

I wish you eternal peace with Almighty God. I hear that the Russians are kind to you and call you to submission. Do not trust them, and do not submit, but have patience. If you are not rewarded in this life, then you will have your reward in the next. Remember what happened before, when your weapons were taken. If then, in 1840, God had not made you see sense, you would already be soldiers, and would go about with bayonets instead of daggers, and your wives would not wear trousers and would be profaned. Judge the future by the past. It is better to die in enmity with the Russians than live with the infidel. Have patience, and I shall come to you with the Koran and a sabre and lead you against the Russians. And for now I strictly forbid you to have not only the intention, but even the idea of submitting to the Russians.

Shamil approved this proclamation and, signing it, resolved to send it out.

After these matters, the business of Hadji Murat was discussed as well. This matter was very important for Shamil. Although he did not even want to admit it, he knew that if Hadji Murat with his cunning, bravery and courage had been with him, what had now happened in Chechnya would not have happened. It would be a good thing to make peace with Hadji Murat and once again make use of his services; but if that were not possible, he could nonetheless not be allowed to help the Russians. And for that reason it was necessary in any event to summon him and, after summoning him, to kill him. The means to this end was either to send a man to Tiflis who would kill him there, or to summon him and put an end to him here. There was only one means for this – his family and, most important, his son, for whom, Shamil knew, Hadji Murat had a passionate love. And for that reason it was necessary to act through his son.

When his advisers had spoken about this, Shamil closed his eyes and fell silent.

His advisers knew that this meant he was now listening to the voice of the Prophet speaking to him, indicating what should be done. After five minutes of solemn silence Shamil opened his eyes, screwed them up even more, and said:

'Bring Hadji Murat's son to me.'

'He is here,' said Jemal Edin.

And indeed, Hadji Murat's son Yusuf, thin, pale, ragged and smelly, but still handsome both in body and face, with just the same fiery, black eyes as his grandmother Patimat, was already standing at the gates of the outer courtyard, awaiting his summons.

Yusuf did not share his father's feelings for Shamil. He did not know all that had happened, or else knew, but, not having lived through it, did not understand why his father was so unyieldingly hostile to Shamil. To him, who wanted only one thing, the continuation of the easy, wild life that he had led in Khunzakh as the son of the governor, it seemed quite unnecessary to be hostile to Shamil. In rebuff and contradiction to his father he had particular admiration for Shamil and felt for him the rapturous worship that was widespread in the mountains. Now with a special feeling of timid awe for the imam he entered the guest-room and, stopping by the door, met with the unyielding, squinting gaze of Shamil. He stood for some time, then went up to Shamil and kissed his large white hand with its long fingers.

'You are Hadji Murat's son?'

'I am, imam.'

'Do you know what he has done?'

'I know, imam, and I regret it.'

'Can you write?'

'I was preparing to become a mullah.'

'Then write to your father that if he comes back to me now, before the festival of Bairam, I shall forgive him, and everything will be as it was before. But if not, and he remains with the Russians, then,' Shamil frowned threateningly, 'I shall give your grandmother and your mother to the villages, and you I shall behead.'

Not a single muscle stirred in Yusuf's face, but he bent his head as a sign that he had understood Shamil's words.

'Write in that vein and give it to my messenger.'

Shamil fell silent and looked at Yusuf for a long time.

'Write that I have taken pity on you and will not kill you, but will put out your eyes, as I do to all traitors. Go.'

Yusuf seemed calm in the presence of Shamil, but when he was taken out of the guest-room, he threw himself upon the man who was leading him and, pulling his dagger from its sheath, tried to cut his own throat with it, but he was seized by the arms, they were tied up and he was led away again to the pit.

That evening, when the evening prayers had ended and it was getting dark, Shamil put on a white fur coat and went out to the other side of the fence to the part of the courtyard where his wives were accommodated, and went in the direction of Aminet's room. But Aminet was not there. She was with the senior wives. Then Shamil, trying not to be noticed, went and stood behind the door to the room to wait for her. But Aminet was angry with Shamil because he had given some silk material not to her, but to Zaidet. She saw him come out and go into her room, looking for her, and she did not go to her room on purpose. She stood for a long time in the doorway of Zaidet's room and, laughing quietly, watched the white figure, now entering, now leaving her room. Having waited for her in vain, Shamil returned to his own room when it was already time for the midnight prayers.

95

20

Hadji Murat lived for a week in the fortress in Ivan Matveyevich's house. Despite the fact that Maria Dmitriyevna quarrelled with shaggy Khanefi (Hadji Murat took only two men with him, Khanefi and Eldar) and once pushed him out of the kitchen, for which he almost cut her throat, she obviously had special feelings of respect and liking for Hadji Murat. She now no longer served him dinner, having passed that task on to Eldar, but took every opportunity to see him and to please him. She also took the most lively interest in the negotiations concerning his family, knew how many wives he had, how many children and of what ages, and after every visit by a scout she would interrogate whomsoever she could about the consequences of the negotiations.

Meanwhile Butler and Hadji Murat became great friends during the week. Sometimes Hadji Murat visited him in his room, sometimes Butler visited him. Sometimes they conversed through an interpreter, and sometimes through their own means, with signs and, most important, smiles. Hadji Murat had obviously taken a liking to Butler. This was clear from Eldar's attitude to Butler. When Butler entered Hadji Murat's room, Eldar greeted Butler, joyfully baring his brilliant teeth, hurriedly put out cushions for him to sit on and took off his sabre, if he was wearing it.

Butler also got to know and became friendly with shaggy Khanefi, Hadji Murat's sworn brother. Khanefi knew many of the songs of the mountaineers and sang them well. To please Butler, Hadji Murat would call Khanefi and order him to sing, choosing the songs that he thought good. Khanefi had a high tenor voice and his singing was unusually distinct and expressive. Hadji Murat liked one of the songs in particular and Butler was struck by its sadly solemn melody. Butler asked the interpreter to tell him what it was about, and noted it down.

The song dealt with a blood feud – the very thing that linked Khanefi and Hadji Murat.

This was the song:

'The earth on my grave will dry, and you will forget me, my dear mother! The graveyard will grow with grass from the grave, the grass will stifle your grief, my old father. The tears will dry on my sister's eyes, and the grief will fly out from her heart.

'But you will not forget me, my eldest brother, until you have avenged my death. Neither will you forget me, my second brother, until you lie down beside me.

'Bullet, you are hot, and you carry death, but were you not my faithful servant? Black earth, you will cover me, but did I not trample you with my steed? You, death, are cold, but I was your lord. The earth will take my body, the sky will take my soul.'

Hadji Murat always listened to this song with his eyes closed, and when it ended with a long drawn-out note that slowly died away, he always said in Russian:

'Good song, wise song.'

With the arrival of Hadji Murat, and his friendship with him and his followers, the poetry of the peculiar, energetic life of the mountaineers took a still greater hold on Butler. He got himself a quilted coat, a Circassian coat and leggings, and it seemed to him that he was himself a mountaineer and that he lived just such a life as these people.

On the day of Hadji Murat's departure, Ivan Matveyevich gathered several officers to give him a send-off. Some of the officers were sitting by the tea-table, where Maria Dmitriyevna was pouring the tea, others by another table with vodka, the strong local wine and food, when Hadji Murat, dressed for the road and wearing his weapons, came limping into the room with quick soft steps.

Everybody stood up and shook hands with him in turn. Ivan Matveyevich invited him to sit on the ottoman, but he thanked him and sat down on a chair by the window. The silence that had fallen at his entrance obviously did not bother him at all. He examined everyone's faces carefully and fixed his indifferent gaze on the table with the samovar and food. A lively officer named Petrokovsky who was seeing Hadji Murat for the first time, asked him through the interpreter whether he had liked Tiflis.

'*Aiya*,' he said.

'He says he did,' replied the interpreter.

'And what did he like?'

Hadji Murat made some reply.

'Most of all he liked the theatre.'

'Well, and did he like it at the commander-in-chief's ball?'

Hadji Murat frowned.

'Every people has its own customs. Our women do not dress like that,' he said, glancing at Maria Dmitriyevna.

'What, didn't he like it?'

'We have a saying,' he said to the interpreter, 'the dog gave meat to the ass, and the ass gave hay to the dog – both went hungry.' He smiled. 'Every people likes its own customs.'

The conversation went no further. Some of the officers began to drink tea, others to eat. Hadji Murat took the glass of tea that was offered him and put it down in front of him.

'Well then? Some cream? A bun?' said Maria Dmitriyevna, serving him.

Hadji Murat bowed his head.

'So it's goodbye, then!' said Butler, tapping him on the knee. 'When will we see one another?'

'Goodbye, goodbye!' said Hadji Murat in Russian, with a smile. '*Kunak bulur*. Strong friend of you. Time, come on, I go,' he said, shaking his head as if in the direction he needed to ride.

In the doorway to the room appeared Eldar with something large and white over his shoulder and with a sabre in his hand. Hadji Murat beckoned to him and Eldar went up to Hadji Murat with his long strides and passed him his white cloak and sabre. Hadji Murat stood up, took the cloak and, throwing it over his arm, passed it to Maria Dmitriyevna and said something to the interpreter. The interpreter said:

'He says: you praised the cloak, so take it.'

'What's this for?' said Maria Dmitriyevna, blushing.

'Must do it. The custom is so,' said Hadji Murat.

'Well I'm grateful,' said Maria Dmitriyevna, taking the cloak. 'God grant you rescue your son. A fine young man,' she added. 'Tell him I hope he rescues his family.'

Hadji Murat glanced at Maria Dmitriyevna and nodded in approval. Then he took the sabre from Eldar's hands and passed it to Ivan Matveyevich. Ivan Matveyevich took the sabre and said to the interpreter:

'Tell him to take my brown gelding, I've nothing else to give him in return.'

Hadji Murat waved his hand in front of his face to show that he needed nothing and would not take it, and then, pointing at the mountains and his heart, he went towards the door. Everyone followed him. The officers who stayed indoors drew the sabre and, examining its blade, decided that it was a genuine *gurda*, a top-quality sword.

Butler went out onto the porch together with Hadji Murat. But at this point something happened that nobody was expecting, and that might have ended with Hadji Murat's death, had it not been for his quick wits, decisiveness and agility.

The inhabitants of the Kumyk village of Tash-Kichu, who had great respect for Hadji Murat and had come to the fort many times just to get a glimpse of the renowned governor, had sent messengers to Hadji Murat three days before his departure to invite him to their mosque on Friday. But when they heard about this, the Kumyk princes living in Tash-Kichu, who hated Hadji Murat and had a blood feud with him, announced to the people that they would not let Hadji Murat into the mosque. The people became restive, and a fight took place between the people and the princes' supporters. The Russian authorities pacified the mountaineers and sent to Hadji Murat to tell him not to go to the mosque. Hadji Murat did not go, and everyone thought that this was the end of the matter.

But at the very moment of Hadji Murat's departure, when he came out onto the porch and the horses were standing by the entrance, up to Ivan Matveyevich's house rode a Kumyk prince familiar to Butler and Ivan Matveyevich, Arslan Khan.

Seeing Hadji Murat, he drew a pistol from his belt and aimed it at Hadji Murat. But Arslan Khan had not had time to shoot before Hadji Murat, despite his limp, had quickly leapt down like a cat from the porch towards Arslan Khan. Arslan Khan shot and missed. But Hadji Murat, running up to him, seized the rein of his horse with one hand, pulled out a dagger with the other, and shouted something in Tatar.

At one and the same moment Butler and Eldar ran up to the enemies and seized them by the arms. Ivan Matveyevich came out too at the shot.

'What do you think you're doing, Arslan, playing such a dirty trick at my house!' he said, when he learnt what was the matter. 'It's not right, brother. Do as you will outside, but why start such butchery at my place?'

Arslan Khan, a little man with a black moustache, all pale and trembling, dismounted, gave Hadji Murat a malicious glance and went off with Ivan Matveyevich into the house. And Hadji Murat returned to the horses, breathing hard and smiling.

'What did he want to kill him for?' asked Butler through the interpreter.

'He says: that is our law,' the interpreter conveyed Hadji Murat's words. 'Arslan must take revenge on him for blood. And that is why he wanted to kill him.'

'Well, and what if he catches up with him on the road?' asked Butler.

Hadji Murat smiled.

'So – he kills, then Allah wills it. Well, goodbye,' he said in Russian once again and, taking hold of the horse's withers, he ran his eyes over everyone seeing him off. His gaze met Maria Dmitriyevna's with affection.

'Goodbye, madam,' he said, addressing her, 'thanks.'

'God grant, God grant you rescue your family,' Maria Dmitriyevna repeated.

He did not understand the words, but he understood her concern for him and nodded to her.

'See you don't forget your friend,' said Butler.

'Tell him I am a faithful friend to him and shall never forget,' he replied through the interpreter and, despite his game leg, no sooner had he touched the stirrup than he had quickly and easily transferred his body to the high saddle and, after adjusting his sabre and feeling with a customary movement for his pistol, with that special, proud, warlike look with which a mountaineer sits on a horse, he rode away from Ivan Matveyevich's house. Khanefi and Eldar also mounted their horses and, bidding a friendly farewell to the hosts and the officers, they trotted after their master.

As always, discussion began of the man who had left.

'A fine fellow!'

'He threw himself at Arslan Khan like a wolf, you know; his face altered completely.'

'He'll do the dirty. He's bound to be a real rogue,' said Petrokovsky.

'God grant us a few more Russian rogues like him,' Maria Dmitriyevna suddenly intervened in annoyance. 'He lived with us for a week, and we saw nothing but good from him,' she said. 'Courteous, intelligent, just.'

'How did you find all that out?'

'I found it out, that's all.'

'Fell for him, eh?' said Ivan Matveyevich, who had come in. 'That's the way of it.'

'So I fell for him. What's it to you? Only why criticise when he's a good man? He's a Tatar, but he's a good man.'

'That's right, Maria Dmitriyevna,' said Butler. 'Good for you, sticking up for him.'

2 1

The life of the inhabitants of the advanced forts on the Chechen line went on as of old. There had been two alarms since then at which the companies had turned out and the Cossacks and militia had galloped around, but on neither occasion could they stop the mountaineers. They had got away, and once in Vozdvizhenskaya eight Cossack horses were driven off while they were being watered, and a Cossack was killed. There had been no raids since the time of the last one when the village was sacked. A major expedition to Great Chechnya was only expected in consequence of the appointment of a new commander of the left flank, Prince Baryatinsky.

Prince Baryatinsky, a friend of the heir to the throne and formerly at the head of the Kabardinsky Regiment, now, immediately upon his arrival in Grozny as commander of the entire left flank, gathered a detachment together with a view to continuing to carry out the sovereign's plans, about which Chernyshov had written to Vorontsov. The detachment gathered in Vozdvizhenskaya and left it for a position in the direction of Kurinskoye. The troops halted there to fell trees.

Young Vorontsov lived in a magnificent canvas tent, and his wife, Maria Vasilyevna, visited the camp and often stayed the night. The relations between Baryatinsky and Maria Vasilyevna were a secret from no one, and for that reason the officers of lower social standing and the soldiers were vulgarly abusive about her, because thanks to her presence in the camp they were dispatched to night-time listening posts. It was common for the mountaineers to bring up guns and fire cannon-balls into a camp. These cannon-balls missed for the most part, and so at any ordinary time no measures were taken against this firing; but in order that the mountaineers could not move their guns up and frighten Maria Vasilyevna, listening posts were sent out. Going to listening posts every night so that a lady was not frightened was insulting and offensive, and Maria Vasilyevna was honoured with curses by the soldiers and those officers not accepted into high society.

Butler came on leave from his fort to visit this detachment, to see his schoolfellows from the Corps des Pages who were gathered there, and those who had served with him both as adjutants and orderlies to the senior officers in the Kurinsky Regiment. From the beginning of his stay he had a great deal of fun. He put up in Poltoratsky's tent and found there many an acquaintance who greeted him joyfully. He also went to see Vorontsov, whom he knew a little because he had served at one time in the same regiment as him. Vorontsov received him very well, presented him to Prince Baryatinsky, and invited him to the farewell lunch he was giving for General Kozlovsky, who had been the commander of the left flank before Baryatinsky.

The lunch was magnificent. Six tents were brought and put up alongside one another. A table was laid that filled their entire length, covered with crockery and bottles. Everything was reminiscent of life in the Guards in St Petersburg. They sat down at the table at two o'clock. In the middle of the table sat on one side Kozlovsky, on the other Baryatinsky. The Vorontsovs sat next to Kozlovsky, the husband to the right, the wife to the left. The entire length of the table on both sides sat the officers of the Kabardinsky and Kurinsky regiments. Butler sat next to Poltoratsky; both chatted merrily and drank with the neighbouring officers. When they got to the roast meat and the batmen began pouring champagne into the glasses, Poltoratsky said to Butler with sincere fear and regret:

'Our "like" is going to disgrace himself.'

'How's that?'

'He needs to make a speech, doesn't he? And is he any good at it?'

'That's right, old fellow, it's not the same as capturing earthworks under fire. And with a lady alongside there as well, and these gentlemen from Court… You really feel sorry, just looking at him,' said the officers amongst themselves.

But then the solemn moment arrived. Baryatinsky stood up and, raising his glass, addressed a short speech to Kozlovsky. When Baryatinsky had finished, Kozlovsky stood up and began in quite a firm voice:

'By the will of His Imperial Majesty I am leaving you, parting with you, gentlemen officers,' he said. 'But consider me always, like, with you… You are, like, familiar, gentlemen, with the truism that the voice of one man is the voice of no one. And so everything with which I have been, like, rewarded during my service, everything that has been, like, showered upon me, for the great generosity of our Sovereign Emperor, like, my entire position and, like, good name – for everything, absolutely everything, like…' – here his voice began to quiver – 'I am, like, indebted to you alone and to you alone, my dear friends!' And his wrinkled face wrinkled still more. He gave a sob, and tears welled up in his eyes. 'With all my heart I offer you, like, my sincere, heartfelt gratitude…'

Kozlovsky could speak no more and, rising, he began embracing the officers who went up to him. Everyone was touched. The Princess covered her face with her handkerchief. Prince Semyon Mikhailovich, twisting his mouth, blinked his eyes. Many of the officers also became tearful. Butler, who scarcely knew Kozlovsky, could not contain his tears either. He found all this extremely pleasing. Then the toasts began, to Baryatinsky, to Vorontsov, to the officers, to the soldiers, and the guests left the dinner intoxicated both by the wine they had drunk and by the military rapture, to which they were in any case particularly inclined.

The weather was wonderful, sunny and calm with bracing fresh air. Camp-fires crackled on all sides, songs could be heard. Everybody seemed to be celebrating something. Butler went to Poltoratsky's in the happiest, most touched frame of mind. Officers gathered at Poltoratsky's, a card table was set up, and an adjutant put up a hundred roubles for the bank. Butler left the tent a couple of times holding his purse in his hand inside his trouser-pocket, but finally he could resist no more and, despite the promise he had made himself and his brothers not to play cards, he began gambling.

And not an hour had passed before Butler, all flushed, sweating and covered in chalk-marks, sat with both elbows on the table, writing the sums of his stakes under cards with crumpled corners and transferred bets[26]. He had lost so much that he was frightened even to add up what was written down as owing from him. Without adding it up he knew that when he had handed over the pay that he could draw in advance, and the value of his horse, he could still not pay everything that he had been noted down as owing by the unfamiliar adjutant. He would still have carried on playing, but, pulling a stern face, the adjutant put the cards down with his clean white hands and began adding up the chalk column of Butler's bets. In embarrassment Butler asked to be forgiven for not being able to pay all that he had lost straight away, and said that he would send it from home, and when he had said this, he noticed that everyone felt sorry for him, and that everyone, even Poltoratsky, was avoiding his glance. This was his last evening. If he had only not gambled, but had gone to Vorontsov's, where he had been invited, 'then things would all have been alright,' he thought. But now not only were they not alright, they were dreadful.

After saying goodbye to his comrades and acquaintances, he rode home and, on arriving, immediately went to bed and slept for an unbroken eighteen hours, as people usually sleep after losing at cards. From the way that he asked her for fifty kopeks to give as a tip to the Cossack who had accompanied him, and from his sad look and brief answers, Maria Dmitriyevna realised that he had lost all his money, and she berated Ivan Matveyevich for letting him go.

The next day Butler woke up after eleven o'clock and, when he remembered his situation, he would have liked to sink once again into the oblivion from which he had just emerged, but he could not. He needed to take measures to pay off the four hundred and seventy roubles that he still owed to a man he did not know. One of these measures consisted in writing a letter to his brother, confessing his wrongdoing, and imploring him to send for the last time five hundred roubles in respect of the mill, which still remained in their joint possession. Then he wrote to a miserly relative of his, asking her to give him, at any rate of interest she liked, the same five hundred roubles. Then he went to Ivan Matveyevich and, knowing that he, or rather Maria Dmitriyevna had some money, asked him for a loan of five hundred roubles.

'I'd give you it,' said Ivan Matveyevich, 'I'd give you it now, but Mashka won't. These women, the devil knows, they're just so tight-fisted. But you must, you really must get yourself out of this mess, damn it! Hasn't that devil of a camp-hawker got it?'

But there was no point in even trying to borrow from the camp-hawker. So Butler's salvation could come only from his brother or from his miserly relative.

22

Without having achieved his objective in Chechnya, Hadji Murat returned to Tiflis and went to see Vorontsov every day, and, when he was received, he begged him to gather together the captive mountaineers and exchange them for his family. Again he said that without this he was tied and could not serve the Russians as he would like and destroy Shamil. Vorontsov made indefinite promises to do what he could, but put things off, saying that he would decide matters when General Argutinsky arrived in Tiflis and he had talked it over with him. Then Hadji Murat began asking Vorontsov to allow him to go and live for a while in Nukha, a small Transcaucasian town, where he supposed it would be more convenient for him to negotiate about his family with Shamil and the people loyal to him. Apart from that, in Nukha, a Muslim town, there was a mosque where he could more conveniently perform the rites of prayer that Muslim law demanded. Vorontsov wrote to St Petersburg about this, but in the meantime allowed Hadji Murat to go to Nukha anyway.

For Vorontsov and for the authorities in St Petersburg, just as for the majority of the Russians who knew Hadji Murat's story, this story was seen either as a fortunate turn in the war in the Caucasus, or simply as an interesting event; but for Hadji Murat, especially in recent times, this was a terrible turning-point in his life. He had fled from the mountains in part to save himself, in part out of hatred for Shamil, and, however hard this flight had been, he had achieved his end, and to begin with he was pleased with his success and did actually consider plans for an attack on Shamil. But it had turned out that his family's departure, which he had thought would be easy to arrange, was in fact more difficult. Shamil had seized his family and, holding them captive, had promised to give the women out to the villages and to kill or blind his son. Now Hadji Murat was moving to Nukha with the intention of trying, through his adherents in Dagestan, to rescue his family from Shamil, either by cunning or by force. The last scout who had been to see him in Nukha had informed him that Avars loyal to him were going to seize his family and come over to the Russians together with them, but that there were too few men prepared to do this and they did not dare to do it in the place where the family was imprisoned, in Vedeno, but would do it only if the family were taken from Vedeno to some other place. In that event they promised to do it on the way. Hadji Murat had his friends told that he promised three thousand roubles for his family's rescue.

In Nukha Hadji Murat was given a small house with five rooms not far from the mosque and the khan's palace. In the same house lived the officers and interpreter attached to him, and his men. Hadji Murat's life passed in awaiting and receiving scouts from the mountains, and riding on horseback, as he was permitted, in the vicinity of Nukha.

On returning from a ride on the 8th of April, Hadji Murat learnt that in his absence an official had arrived from Tiflis. Despite all his desire to find out what the official had brought him, before going to the room where the official and a police officer were waiting for him, Hadji Murat went to his room and carried out the midday prayer ceremony. When he had finished praying, he went out into the other room that served as drawing-room and reception room. The official who had come from Tiflis, a fat little state councillor, Kirillov, conveyed to Hadji Murat Vorontsov's desire that he should come back to Tiflis by the 12th for a meeting with Argutinsky.

'*Yakshi*,' said Hadji Murat, angrily.

He did not like the official, Kirillov.

'And you brought money?'

'I have,' said Kirillov.

'For two weeks now,' said Hadji Murat, and showed ten fingers and then four more. 'Hand over.'

'We'll hand it over in a moment,' said the official, taking a purse from his travelling bag. 'And what does he need the money for?' he said in Russian to the police officer, supposing that Hadji Murat did not understand, but Hadji Murat understood and looked at Kirillov angrily. While he was getting the money out, Kirillov, who wanted to get into conversation with Hadji Murat so as to have something to tell Vorontsov upon his return, asked him through the interpreter whether it was dull for him here. Hadji Murat gave the fat little man in civilian dress and without weapons a sidelong, contemptuous glance, and made no reply. The interpreter repeated the question.

'Tell him I do not want to talk to him. Let him hand over the money.'

And saying this, Hadji Murat sat down again at the table, preparing to count the money.

When Kirillov had taken out the gold coins and set out seven piles of ten roubles each (Hadji Murat received five roubles a day), he moved them towards Hadji Murat. Hadji Murat poured the gold coins into the sleeve of his Circassian coat, stood up, and quite unexpectedly slapped the state councillor on the shoulder before setting off out of the room. The state councillor leapt up and told the interpreter to say that he should not dare to do that, because he held the rank of a colonel. The police officer also confirmed that this was so. But Hadji Murat nodded his head as a sign that he knew and left the room.

'What can you do with him?' said the police officer. 'He'll stick a dagger in you, and that's that. You can't talk to these devils. I can see he's beginning to go mad.'

As soon as it got dark, two scouts arrived from the mountains with hoods drawn over their faces as far as the eyes. A police officer led them through to Hadji Murat's rooms. One of the scouts was a fleshy, dark Tavlin, the other a thin old man. The news they had brought was joyless for Hadji Murat. His friends who had taken it upon themselves to rescue his family now refused outright to do so, fearing Shamil, who threatened those helping Hadji Murat with the most terrible punishments. After hearing out the scouts' story, Hadji Murat propped his elbows on his crossed legs and, lowering his head in his sheepskin hat, was silent for a long time. Hadji Murat was thinking, and thinking decisively. He knew that he was thinking now for the last time, and that a decision was essential. Hadji Murat raised his head and, taking out two gold coins, he gave one to each of the scouts and said:

'Go.'

'What reply will there be?'

'The reply will be the one God gives. Go.'

The scouts stood up and left, but Hadji Murat continued to sit on the carpet, resting his elbows on his knees. He sat like this, thinking, for a long time.

'What can I do? Trust Shamil and return to him?' thought Hadji Murat. 'He is a fox – he will deceive me. And even if he did not deceive me, I could not submit to him, the red-haired trickster. I could not, because now, after I have spent time with the Russians, he will no longer trust me,' thought Hadji Murat.

And he recalled the Tavlin folk-tale of the falcon which was caught, lived with people, and then returned to its own kind in the mountains. It returned, but in chains, and bells remained on the chains. And the falcons did not accept it. 'Fly away,' they said, 'to the place where they put silver bells on you. We have no bells, and no chains either.' The falcon did not want to quit its birthplace and stayed. But the other falcons would not accept it and pecked it to death.

'In this way they will peck me to death also,' thought Hadji Murat.

'Remain here? Subjugate the Caucasus to the Russian Tsar, earn glory, rank, wealth?… That is a possibility,' he thought, remembering his meetings with Vorontsov and the flattering words of the old Prince.

'But I need to decide now, or else he will destroy my family.'

All night long Hadji Murat stayed awake, thinking.

23

By the middle of the night his decision was made. He decided that he should escape to the mountains and burst into Vedeno with the Avars loyal to him and either free his family or die. Whether he would bring his family back over to the Russians or flee with it to Khunzakh and carry on the struggle with Shamil, that he did not decide. He knew only that now he needed to escape from the Russians into the mountains. And now he began to carry out this decision. He took his black quilted coat from beneath his pillow and went into his men's quarters. They were staying on the far side of the entrance-lobby. As soon as he went out into the lobby with its open door, he was gripped by the dewy freshness of the moonlit night and his ears were struck by the whistles and trilling of several nightingales at once from the garden adjoining the house.

Passing through the lobby, Hadji Murat opened the door into his men's room. There was no light in this room, only the new moon in its first quarter shone through the windows. A table and two chairs stood to one side, and all four men were lying on rugs and felt cloaks on the floor. Khanefi slept outside with the horses. Gamzalo, hearing the creak of the door, sat up, looked around at Hadji Murat and, recognising him, lay down again. But Eldar, who was lying alongside, leapt up and began putting on his quilted coat, awaiting orders. Kurban and Khan Magoma slept. Hadji Murat put his quilted coat on the table, and something hard in the coat struck against the boards of the table. It was the gold coins sewn into it.

'Sew these in too,' said Hadji Murat, handing the gold coins he had received that day to Eldar.

Eldar took the coins and, stepping into a bright spot, he immediately took a little knife from beneath his dagger and began slitting the lining of the coat. Gamzalo sat up and remained sitting with his legs crossed.

'And you, Gamzalo, tell the men to inspect their rifles and pistols and prepare their charges. We shall ride a long way tomorrow,' said Hadji Murat.

'We have powder, we have bullets. All will be ready,' said Gamzalo, and started growling something incomprehensible.

Gamzalo realised why Hadji Murat was ordering rifles to be loaded. From the very beginning he had desired one thing, and the further things went, the stronger and stronger was the desire: to kill and slaughter as many Russian dogs as possible and escape to the mountains. And now he could see that Hadji Murat wanted this very thing too, and he was pleased.

When Hadji Murat had gone, Gamzalo woke his comrades up, and all four of them spent the whole night looking over rifles, pistols, touch-holes, flints, replacing bad ones, pouring fresh powder into pans, filling cartridge-pouches with measured charges of powder and bullets wrapped in oily rags, sharpening sabres and daggers and rubbing the blades with pork fat.

Hadji Murat went out into the lobby again a little before dawn to get some water for his ablutions. In the lobby the singing of the nightingales before the light could be heard even more loudly and frequently than in the evening. But in his men's room could be heard the rhythmic hissing and whistling of the iron on stone of a dagger being sharpened. Hadji Murat scooped some water out of the tub and had already reached his own door when he heard in his followers' room, besides the noise of the sharpening, Khanefi's reedy voice as well, singing a song familiar to Hadji Murat. Hadji Murat stopped and began to listen.

The song told of how the horseman Gamzat and his men drove off a herd of white horses from the Russian side, and of how he was then caught beyond the River Terek by a Russian prince, who surrounded him with an army like a forest. Then it sang of how Gamzat killed the horses and sat with his men behind a bloody rampart of dead horses and fought with the Russians while bullets still remained in their rifles, daggers in their belts and blood in their veins. But before dying, Gamzat caught sight of some birds in the sky and shouted to them: 'You, migrating birds, fly to our homes and tell our sisters, mothers and white-skinned maidens, that we all died for the Holy War. Tell them our bodies will not lie in graves, but our bones will be torn apart and gnawed by greedy wolves and our eyes pecked out by black ravens.'

With these words the song ended, and joining in with these final words, sung to a mournful tune, was the lively voice of cheerful Khan Magoma, who at the very end of the song shouted loudly 'Lya illyakha il Allah' and gave a piercing shriek. Then all fell quiet, and again there could be heard only the smacking and whistles of the nightingales from the garden, and the rhythmic hissing and occasional whistling of iron slipping quickly over stone from behind the door.

Hadji Murat was so immersed in thought that he did not notice how he had tipped the jug and the water had poured out of it. He shook his head at himself and went into his room.

After carrying out his morning prayer, Hadji Murat inspected his weapons and sat down on his bed. There was nothing more to do. In order to ride out, he needed to ask permission of the police officer. But it was still dark outside, and the police officer was still asleep.

Khanefi's song had reminded him of another song, composed by his mother. This song told of something that had really happened, happened when Hadji Murat had only just been born, but about which his mother had told him.

The song went like this:

'Your damask steel dagger tore my white breast apart, but to it I clasped my sunshine, my boy, washed him with my hot blood, and the wound healed without herbs and roots, I did not fear death, and my horseman-son will not fear it either.'

The words of this song were addressed to Hadji Murat's father, and the meaning of the song was that when Hadji Murat was born, the khan's wife also gave birth to her second son, Umma Khan, and demanded that Hadji Murat's mother, who had fed her elder son Abununtsal, should come to her as a wet-nurse. But Patimat did not want to leave this son and said she would not go. Hadji Murat's father grew angry and ordered her. And when she again refused, he struck her with a dagger and would have killed her if she had not been taken away. And so she did not give him up, but finished feeding him, and composed a song about it all.

Hadji Murat recalled how his mother, when putting him to sleep alongside her under a fur coat on the roof of the hut, sang him this song, and he asked her to show him the place on her side where the scar of the wound remained. He saw his mother before him as if she were real – not so lined and grey, with a lattice of teeth as he had left her now, but young, pretty, and so strong that when he was already about five and heavy, she carried him across the mountains to see his grandfather in a basket on her back.

And he remembered his wrinkled grandfather with a little grey beard too, a silversmith, and how he chased the silver with his sinewy hands and made his grandson say his prayers. He remembered the fountain down the hill where he would go with his mother for water, holding on to her trousers. He remembered the thin dog that licked his face, and especially the smell and taste of smoke and sour milk when he went to fetch his mother from the shed where she milked the cow and baked the milk. He remembered how his mother shaved his head for the first time and how in the shiny copper bowl hanging on the wall he saw in wonderment his little round head showing blue.

And recalling himself when he was little, he also recalled his beloved son Yusuf, whose head he had himself shaved for the first time. Now this Yusuf was already a handsome young horseman. He recalled his son as he had seen him last. It was on the day he was riding out of Tselmes. His son brought him his horse and asked permission to go with him. He was dressed and armed and was holding his own horse by the reins. Yusuf's ruddy, young, handsome face and the whole of his tall, slim figure (he was taller than his father) breathed the courage of youth and the joy of life. His shoulders, broad in spite of his youth, his very broad, adolescent pelvis and his long, slim torso, his long, powerful arms, and the strength, agility and dexterity in all his movements always pleased his father, and he always admired his son.

'Better stay. You are on your own in the house now. Keep your mother and grandmother safe,' said Hadji Murat.

And Hadji Murat could remember the expression of mettle and pride with which, flushed with pleasure, Yusuf said that, while he lived, nobody would do harm to his mother and grandmother. Nonetheless, Yusuf mounted his horse and went with his father as far as the stream. He turned back from the stream, and since then Hadji Murat had not seen either his wife, his mother or his son.

And this was the son that Shamil wanted to blind! Of what would be done to his wife, he did not even want to think.

These thoughts so agitated Hadji Murat that he could not remain seated any longer. He jumped up and, limping, quickly went up to the door, opened it and called for Eldar. The sun was not yet rising, but it was fully light. The nightingales had not stopped their singing.

'Go and tell the police officer that I wish to go out for a ride, and saddle the horses,' he said.

24

Butler's sole consolation at this time was the poetry of war to which he devoted himself not only in his service, but also in his private life. Dressed in Circassian costume he showed off his horsemanship, and twice took part in ambushes with Bogdanovich, although on both these occasions they caught nobody and killed nobody. This bravery and friendship with the well-known daredevil Bogdanovich seemed to Butler pleasant and important. He had paid off his debt by borrowing the money from a Jew at a huge rate of interest, that is he had simply delayed and put off an unresolved situation. He tried not to think of his position and, besides the poetry of war, he also tried to achieve oblivion through wine. He drank more and more, and from day to day he grew more and more morally weak. He was now no longer the fine Joseph[27] in relation to Maria Dmitriyevna, but on the contrary began making crude advances to her, yet, to his surprise, he met with a decisive rebuff, which shamed him greatly.

At the end of April a detachment that Baryatinsky had earmarked for a new movement through the whole of what was considered impassable Chechnya came to the fort. Here were two companies of the Kabardinsky Regiment, and these companies, in accordance with the established Caucasian tradition, were received as guests by the companies stationed in Kurinskoye. The soldiers were distributed between the barracks and entertained not only with supper, porridge and beef, but also with vodka, and the officers were placed with various officers and, as was the custom, the local officers entertained the visitors.

The entertainment ended with a drinking-bout with the regimental singers, and Ivan Matveyevich, very drunk and no longer red, but pale-grey, sat mounted on a chair and, drawing his sabre, hacked with it at imaginary enemies, by turns cursing, chuckling, embracing people, and dancing to his favourite song: 'Shamil began to mutiny in years gone by, trai-rai-ratatai, in years gone by.'

Butler was here too. He tried to see the poetry of war in this as well, but in the depths of his soul he felt sorry for Ivan Matveyevich, yet there was absolutely no chance of stopping him. And Butler, feeling the drink in his head, quietly slipped out and went home.

The full moon shone on the little white houses and the stones of the road. It was so light that every little pebble, wisp of straw and animal dropping could be seen on the road. Approaching the house, Butler met Maria Dmitriyevna wearing a shawl that covered her head and shoulders. After the rebuff that Maria Dmitriyevna had given Butler, he felt rather ashamed and had been avoiding meeting her. But now, in the moonlight and because of the wine he had drunk, Butler was glad of this meeting and tried to be affectionate with her.

'Where are you going?' he asked.

'To see my old man,' she replied, amicably. She had rejected Butler's advances absolutely sincerely and decisively, but she found it unpleasant that he had been shunning her all the time recently.

'Why go and see him, he'll come home.'

'But will he though?'

'If he doesn't come, he'll be carried.'

'That's just it, and after all, that's not a good thing,' said Maria Dmitriyevna. 'So I shouldn't go?'

'No, don't go. Let's go home instead.'

Maria Dmitriyevna turned round and set off for home alongside Butler. The moon was shining so brightly that there was a radiance moving around the head of the shadow that moved by the side of the road. Butler looked at this radiance around his head and was going to tell her that he still liked her just as much, but did not know how to begin. She waited to hear what he would say. Thus, in silence, they were already very nearly home when some horsemen rode out from around a corner. It was an officer with an escort.

'Who's that God's bringing us?' said Maria Dmitriyevna, and stepped aside.

The moon was shining from behind the new arrival so that Maria Dmitriyevna recognised him only when he had drawn almost level with them. It was Kamenev, an officer who had previously served together with Ivan Matveyevich, and so Maria Dmitriyevna knew him.

'Pyotr Nikolayevich, is it you?' Maria Dmitriyevna said to him.

'The very same,' said Kamenev. 'Ah, Butler! Hello! Not asleep yet? Having a walk with Maria Dmitriyevna? Look out, Ivan Matveyevich'll give you what for! Where is he?'

'Can't you hear?' said Maria Dmitriyevna, indicating the direction from which there carried the sounds of a bass drum and a song. 'They're having a binge.'

'What's that then, your lot bingeing?'

'No, some men have come from Khasav-Yurt, so they're being entertained.'

'Ah, that's good. I'll be in time too. I've only come to see him for a minute.'

'What, some business is there?' asked Butler.

'There's a little matter, yes.'

'Good or bad?'

'That depends! Good for us, rotten for someone else,' Kamenev laughed.

At this point, both those on foot and Kamenev came up to Ivan Matveyevich's house.

'Chikhirev!' called Kamenev to a Cossack. 'Ride up!'

A Don Cossack moved out from the remainder and rode up. He was in the ordinary uniform of a Don Cossack, wearing boots and a greatcoat, and with saddle-bags behind his saddle.

'Well, get the thing out,' said Kamenev, dismounting.

The Cossack dismounted too and took a sack containing something out of a saddle-bag. Kamenev took the sack from the Cossack's hands and put his own hand inside.

'So, shall I show you the news? You won't be frightened?' he said to Maria Dmitriyevna.

'Why should I be afraid?' said Maria Dmitriyevna.

'Here it is,' said Kamenev, taking out a human head and holding it up in the light of the moon. 'Recognise it?'

It was a shaved head, with large protuberances on the skull above the eyes and a trimmed black beard and clipped moustache, with one eye open and one half-closed, with a shaven skull that had been hacked open but not completely so, and a nose, covered in dried black blood. The neck was wrapped in a blood-soaked towel. Despite the wounds on the head, in the line of the blue lips there was a kind, childlike expression.

Maria Dmitriyevna looked and, without saying a thing, turned and went away into the house with rapid strides.

Butler could not take his eyes off the terrible head. It was the head of the same Hadji Murat with whom he had so recently spent evenings in such friendly conversation.

'How can this be? Who killed him? Where?' he asked.

'He tried to get away and was caught,' said Kamenev, and gave the head back to the Cossack, then himself went into the house together with Butler.

'And he died like a hero,' said Kamenev.

'But how did it all happen?'

'Just wait, and when Ivan Matveyevich arrives, I'll tell you everything in detail. That's why I was sent, after all. I'm taking it round all the forts and villages and displaying it.'

Ivan Matveyevich was sent for, and he returned to the house, drunk, with two officers who had been drinking just as heavily, and set about embracing Kamenev.

'I've brought you Hadji Murat's head,' said Kamenev.

'Nonsense! Has he been killed?'

'Yes, he tried to escape.'

'I said he'd do the dirty. So where is it, then? The head? Come on, show us!'

The Cossack was called and he brought in the sack with the head. The head was taken out, and Ivan Matveyevich looked at it for a long time with drunken eyes.

'But he was a good fellow, anyway,' he said. 'Let me give him a kiss.'

'Yes, it's true, he had a good head on him,' said one of the officers.

When everyone had inspected the head, it was given back to the Cossack again. The Cossack put the head in the sack, trying to lower it to the floor in such a way that it banged against it as gently as possible.

'Well and what do you say, Kamenev, every time you show it?' said one of the officers.

'No, let me give him a kiss. He gave me a sabre,' shouted Ivan Matveyevich.

Butler went out onto the porch. Maria Dmitriyevna was sitting on the second step. She glanced round at Butler and immediately turned away angrily.

'What's the matter, Maria Dmitriyevna?' asked Butler.

'You're all cutthroats. I can't stand it. Just cutthroats,' she said, getting up.

'The same thing could happen to anyone,' said Butler, not knowing what to say. 'That's what war's about.'

'War!' cried Maria Dmitriyevna. 'What war? Cutthroats, and that's all. A dead body should be committed to the ground, but they stand there grinning. Just cutthroats,' she repeated, stepped down from the porch and went off into the house by the back entrance.

Butler returned to the drawing-room and asked Kamenev to tell them in detail how it had all happened.

And Kamenev told them.

This was how it had happened.

25

Hadji Murat was permitted to go riding in the vicinity of the town, but only with an escort of Cossacks. In all there was about half a squadron of Cossacks in Nukha, of whom ten or so were distributed among the high-ranking officials, while the remainder, if they were to be sent out, as ordered, ten at a time, would have had to be detailed every other day. And so on the first day there were ten Cossacks sent out, but afterwards it was decided to send five at a time, with the request that Hadji Murat should not take all his men with him, but on the 25th of April Hadji Murat went out on his ride with all five. As Hadji Murat was mounting his horse, the military commander noticed that all five men intended to ride with Hadji Murat, and told him that he was not allowed to take them all with him, but Hadji Murat did not seem to hear; he set his horse moving, and the military commander did not insist. With the Cossacks was a non-commissioned officer, a holder of the Cross of St George, a strapping brown-haired young fellow, with a pudding-basin haircut and a healthy complexion, Nazarov. He was the eldest in a poor family of Old Believers[28] who had grown up without a father and who was the breadwinner for his old mother with her three daughters and two brothers.

'See you don't let him go far, Nazarov!' called the military commander.

'No, Your Honour,' replied Nazarov and, raising himself in his stirrups, he set his good, big, hook-nosed, chestnut gelding off at a trot, holding onto the rifle over his shoulder. Behind him rode four Cossacks: Ferapontov, lanky, thin, number one thief and procurer – the very one that had sold powder to Gamzalo; Ignatov, who was coming to the end of his term of service, not a young man, a strapping peasant who boasted of his strength; Mishkin, a weedy teenager who was mocked by everyone; and Petrakov, young and fair-haired, his mother's only son, always affectionate and cheerful.

The early morning was misty, but by breakfast time the weather had cleared up and the sun was shining on the newly opened foliage, and on the young virgin grass, and on the cereal shoots, and on the ripples of the fast-flowing river which could be seen to the left of the road.

Hadji Murat rode at walking pace. The Cossacks and his men followed behind him at the same speed. They rode out along the road behind the fortress. They met women with baskets on their heads, soldiers on wagons, and creaking carts drawn by buffaloes. When they had gone a couple of kilometres, Hadji Murat touched his white Kabardian horse on, and it extended its stride so that his men continued at a fast trot. The Cossacks did the same too.

'Hey, that's a good horse he's got under him,' said Ferapontov. 'If he wasn't on our side now, I'd have him off it.'

'Yes, mate, they were offering three hundred roubles for that horse in Tiflis.'

'But I'll catch him on mine,' said Nazarov.

'Of course you will,' said Ferapontov.

Hadji Murat kept on increasing his pace.

'Hey, friend, you mustn't do that. Take it easy!' cried Nazarov, catching up with Hadji Murat.

Hadji Murat looked back and, saying nothing, continued riding at the same canter, without lessening his pace.

'Look what they're up to, the devils,' said Ignatov. 'See, they're getting away.'

They went on like this for about a kilometre in the direction of the mountains.

'I tell you, you mustn't!' Nazarov shouted again.

Hadji Murat did not reply and did not look back, only increased his pace still more and moved on from a canter to a gallop.

'No you don't, you won't get away!' cried Nazarov, stung to the quick.

He struck his big chestnut gelding with his whip and, half rising in his stirrups and leaning forward, set him off at full pelt after Hadji Murat.

The sky was so clear, the air so fresh, the forces of life played so joyously in Nazarov's soul when, merging into one being with his good, strong horse, he flew across the level ground after Hadji Murat, that the possibility of something bad, sad or terrible never even entered his mind. He was happy that with every stride he was gaining on Hadji Murat and getting closer to him. Hadji Murat realised from the clattering hooves of the Cossack's big horse getting closer to him that he must soon be caught, and, taking hold of his pistol with his right hand, he began with his left slightly to restrain his excited Kabardian, who could hear the clattering of a horse behind him.

'You mustn't, I tell you!' cried Nazarov, almost drawing alongside Hadji Murat, and reaching out a hand to seize the rein of his horse. But he did not manage to seize the rein before a shot rang out.

'What are you doing?' shouted Nazarov, clutching at his chest. 'Kill them, lads,' he said and, swaying, slumped onto the pommel of his saddle.

But the mountaineers took hold of their weapons before the Cossacks, shot the Cossacks with their pistols and hacked them with their sabres. Nazarov hung on the neck of his frightened horse, which carried him in circles around his comrades. Ignatov's horse fell beneath him, trapping his leg. Two of the mountaineers, pulling out their sabres and without dismounting, slashed him across the head and arms. Petrakov was about to rush towards his comrade, but straight away two shots seared him, one in the back, the other in the side, and, like a sack, he tumbled from his horse.

Mishkin turned his horse back and galloped towards the fortress. Khanefi and Khan Magoma sped after Mishkin, but he was already a long way ahead, and the mountaineers could not catch him.

Seeing that they could not catch the Cossack, Khanefi and Khan Magoma returned to their friends. Gamzalo, after finishing Ignatov off with his dagger, threw Nazarov from his horse and cut his throat too. Khan Magoma took the dead men's bags of cartridges. Khanefi wanted to take Nazarov's horse, but Hadji Murat called to him not to, and set off down the road ahead. His followers galloped after him, driving away Petrakov's horse which was running after them. They were already among fields of rice three kilometres from Nukha when a shot rang out from the tower, signalling the alarm.

Petrakov lay on his back with his stomach cut open, and his young face was turned towards the sky, and he died, sobbing like a fish.

'Good Lord, oh my forefathers, what have they done!' cried the commander of the fortress, holding his head in his hands, when he learnt of Hadji Murat's escape. 'I'll swing for them! They've let him get away, the villains!' he shouted, listening to Mishkin's report.

The alarm was raised everywhere, and not only were all available Cossacks sent after the fugitives, but in addition all the militiamen from friendly villages who could be gathered were gathered. A reward of a thousand roubles was announced for the man who brought in Hadji Murat, dead or alive. And two hours after Hadji Murat and his comrades had galloped away from the Cossacks, more than two hundred horsemen were galloping after the police officer to seek out and try to catch the fugitives.

After riding several kilometres along the main road, Hadji Murat reined in his white horse, which was breathing hard and had turned grey with sweat, and stopped. To the right of the road could be seen the huts and the minaret of the village of Belardzhik, to the left were fields, and where they ended could be seen a river. Despite the fact that the way into the mountains lay to the right, Hadji Murat turned in the opposite direction, to the left, counting on the pursuit actually racing after him to the right. He, meanwhile, crossing the River Alazan away from the road, would come out onto a highway where nobody would be expecting him, and would ride along it as far as the forest; and only then, after crossing the river once more, would he make his way through the forest into the mountains. When this had been decided, he turned to the left. But it proved impossible to reach the river. The rice field which had to be crossed had just been filled with water, as is always the way in spring, and had turned into a quagmire in which the horses sank above their pasterns. Hadji Murat and his men went to the right and to the left, thinking that they would find a drier spot, but the field they had come upon had been entirely evenly filled and was now saturated with water. The horses pulled their sinking legs from the clinging mud with the noise of popping corks and, after going a few paces, they would stop, breathing hard.

They struggled like this for so long that it was beginning to get dark and they had still not reached the river. To the left was a little islet with the spreading leaves of some bushes, and Hadji Murat decided to ride into these bushes and stay there until nightfall, letting the exhausted horses rest.

When they had ridden into the bushes, Hadji Murat and his men dismounted from their horses and, hobbling them, set them loose to feed, while they themselves ate the bread and cheese they had brought with them. The new moon, which had been shining at first, went down behind the mountains, and the night was dark. There were especially large numbers of nightingales in Nukha. There were two in these bushes as well. While Hadji Murat and his men were making a noise, riding in among the bushes, the nightingales fell silent. But when the men became quiet, they again began trilling, calling to one another. Hadji Murat, listening intently to the sounds of the night, involuntarily listened to them.

And their whistling reminded him of that song about Gamzat which he had listened to the previous night when he had gone out for water. At any minute now he might be in the same position as that in which Gamzat had been. He had the idea that that was how it would be, and he suddenly felt grave in his heart. He spread his cloak out and performed the rite of prayer. And scarcely had he finished it before sounds began to be heard approaching the bushes. These were the sounds of a large number of horses' legs, splashing through the quagmire. Quick-eyed Khan Magoma ran out to one edge of the thicket and made out in the darkness the black shadows of horsemen and men on foot, coming towards the bushes. Khanefi caught sight of just such a crowd on the other side. It was Karganov, the district military commander, with his militiamen.

'Well then, we shall fight like Gamzat,' thought Hadji Murat.

After the alarm had been raised, Karganov hurried in pursuit of Hadji Murat with a squadron of militiamen and Cossacks, but nowhere could he find either him or his trail. Karganov was already returning home, his hopes dashed, when, with evening coming on, he met an old Tatar. Karganov asked the old man whether he had seen a group of six horsemen. The old man replied that he had. He had seen six horsemen meandering through a rice field and riding into the bushes in which he collected firewood. Taking the old man with him, Karganov turned back again and, convinced by the look of the hobbled horses that Hadji Murat was here, he surrounded the bushes while it was still night-time, and set about awaiting the morning to take Hadji Murat dead or alive.

Realising that he was surrounded, Hadji Murat located an old ditch in the middle of the bushes, and resolved to ensconce himself in it and defend himself while he had the cartridges and the strength. He told his comrades this and ordered them to make a barricade in the ditch. His men immediately set about chopping branches, digging the ground with their daggers, making a rampart. Hadji Murat worked along with them.

No sooner had it begun to grow light, than the squadron commander rode up close to the bushes and shouted:

'Hey! Hadji Murat! Surrender! There are many of us, and few of you.'

In reply to this a puff of smoke appeared from the ditch, a rifle cracked, and a bullet hit the militiaman's horse, which shied beneath him and started to fall. After this the rifles of the militiamen standing at the edge of the bushes began to crackle, and their bullets, whistling and buzzing, knocked down leaves and branches and hit the barricade, but failed to hit the people sitting behind the barricade. Only Gamzalo's horse, which had strayed away from the rest, was injured by them. The horse was wounded in the head. It did not fall, but, ripping its hobble apart and crashing through the bushes, it hurried to the other horses and, pressing up against them, poured blood onto the young grass. Hadji Murat and his men fired only when one of the militiamen came on ahead, and they rarely missed the target. Three of the militiamen were wounded, and not only were the militiamen unable to make up their minds to rush Hadji Murat and his men, they were actually moving further and further away from him and firing only from a distance, at random.

Things continued like this for more than an hour. The sun had climbed to half the height of the trees, and Hadji Murat was already thinking of mounting the horses and trying to break through to the river, when the cries of a newly arrived large group were heard. This was Hadji Aga with his men from Mekhtula. There were about two hundred of them. Hadji Aga had once been a special friend of Hadji Murat and lived with him in the mountains, but then he had gone over to the Russians. With him too was Akhmet Khan, the son of an enemy of Hadji Murat. Hadji Aga began, just like Karganov, by shouting to Hadji Murat that he should surrender, but, just as on the first occasion, Hadji Murat replied with a gunshot.

'With sabres, men!' cried Hadji Aga, drawing his own, and the voices of hundreds of men rang out as they rushed, shrieking, into the bushes.

The militiamen ran into the bushes, but from behind the barricade several shots cracked out one after another. Two or three men fell, the attackers halted, and they also began firing from the edge of the thicket. They fired and at the same time gradually approached the barricade, running from bush to bush. Some ran quickly enough, while some fell under the bullets of Hadji Murat and his men. Hadji Murat did not miss a shot, just as rarely did Gamzalo waste one, and he shrieked with joy every time he saw that his bullets had hit. Kurban sat on the edge of the ditch singing '*Lya illyakha il Allah*' and firing unhurriedly, but he rarely hit. Eldar was trembling all over in his impatience to throw himself upon the enemy with his dagger, and he fired often and haphazardly, continually looking round at Hadji Murat and poking his head up from behind the barricade. Hairy Khanefi, with his sleeves rolled up, carried out his role as servant even here. He loaded the rifles that Hadji Murat and Kurban handed him, diligently driving home with an iron ramrod the bullets wrapped in oiled rags and pouring dry powder from a powder-flask into the pans. Khan Magoma did not sit in the ditch like the others, but ran back and forth between the ditch and the horses, driving them to a safer spot, and continually shrieked and fired from the arm without support for the barrel. He was wounded first. The bullet hit him in the neck, and he sat down backwards,

123

spitting blood and cursing. Then Hadji Murat was wounded. The bullet went through his shoulder. Hadji Murat tore some wadding from his felt cloak, plugged his wound and continued firing.

'Let's attack them with sabres,' said Eldar, for the third time.

He poked his head out from behind the barricade, ready to throw himself upon the enemy, but at the same moment a bullet struck him, and he swayed and fell on his back onto Hadji Murat's leg. Hadji Murat glanced at him. His beautiful sheep's eyes looked at Hadji Murat fixedly and seriously. His mouth with the jutting upper lip like that of a child twitched without opening. Hadji Murat freed his leg from beneath him and continued to take aim. Khanefi bent over the dead Eldar and began quickly taking the unused cartridges from his Circassian coat. Kurban meanwhile kept on singing, slowly loading and taking aim.

The enemy, running from bush to bush with whooping and shrieks, moved closer and closer. Another bullet hit Hadji Murat in the left side. He lay down in the ditch and again, tearing a piece of wadding from his felt cloak, he plugged the wound. The wound in his side was fatal, and he felt that he was dying. Memories and images replaced one another in his imagination with extraordinary speed. Now he saw before him mighty Abununtsal Khan as, with one hand holding the hanging cheek that had been chopped off, he threw himself with dagger in hand upon his enemy; now he saw the weak, bloodless old man Vorontsov with his cunning white face and heard his soft voice; now he saw his son, Yusuf, now his wife Sofyat; now the pale face with a red beard and screwed-up eyes of his enemy Shamil.

And all these memories sped by in his imagination without arousing any feeling in him; neither pity, nor malice, nor any desire. All this seemed so insignificant in comparison with what was beginning and had already begun for him. But in the meantime his strong body was continuing with what had been started. He gathered the last of his strength, raised himself from behind the barricade, fired his pistol at a man running towards him, and hit him. The man fell. Then he climbed out of the hole altogether and went with his dagger, limping badly, directly towards his enemies. Several shots rang out, he swayed and fell. Several militiamen with a triumphant shriek rushed towards the fallen body. But what had seemed to them a dead body suddenly began to move. At first the bloodied, shaven, hatless head was raised, then the trunk was raised, then, seizing hold of a tree, he raised the whole of himself. He seemed so terrible that the men running towards him stopped. But suddenly he faltered, staggered away from the tree, and from his full height, like a thistle that has been cut down, he fell onto his face and moved no more.

He did not move, but could still feel. When Hadji Aga, the first to run up to him, struck him on the head with a large dagger, it seemed to him that he was being hit on the head with a hammer, and he could not understand who was doing it and why. This was his last consciousness of a connection with his body. He no longer felt any more, and his enemies trampled and cut something that no longer had anything in common with him. Hadji Aga, with one foot on the body's back, cut off the head with two blows, and carefully, so as not to stain his slippers with blood, rolled it away with his foot. Crimson blood gushed from the artery in the neck and black blood from the head, pouring all over the grass.

Karganov and Hadji Aga and Akhmet Khan and all the militiamen gathered, like a hunter over a dead beast, over the bodies of Hadji Murat and his men (Khanefi, Kurban and Gamzalo were tied up), and the men standing in the powder smoke in the bushes, conversing cheerfully, celebrated their victory.

The nightingales, which had fallen silent during the shooting, began trilling again, one nearby at first, and then others at the far end.

It was of this death that I was reminded by the crushed thistle in the middle of the ploughed-up field.

NOTES

1. As imam, Shamil (*c.*1798–1871) led the resistance to Russian rule in the Caucasus until his surrender in 1859.

2. 'Well, are you going to tell me what it is?'
'But my dear…'
'None of that "my dear"! It's a scout, isn't it?'
'All the same, I can't tell you.'
'You can't? Then I shall have to tell you.'
'You?'

3. 'It's a valuable object.'

4. 'We'll have to find an opportunity to give him a present.'

5. 'Here's the opportunity. Give him the watch.'

6. 'You would do much better to stay; it's my business and not yours.'
'You can't prevent me from going to see the general's wife.'

7. The saying Maria Vasilyevna has in mind is actually 'a bad peace is better than a good quarrel'.

8. The battle in which Vorontsov played a prominent part took place on 7 March 1814 near Laon in the Aisne region of France.

9. 'Excellent, my dear… Simon has had a slice of luck.'

10. 'How awful!'

11. War is war.

12. The name of Napoleon's marshal, Joachim Murat (1767–1815), is pronounced in Russian identically to that of Hadji Murat.

13. 'All this is thanks to you.'

14. Simon was in the wrong. (The Shakespearean quote is delivered in English in the original text.)

15. An offshoot of Sufism, in which a *murid*, or disciple, is shown the path to spiritual enlightenment by a *murshid*, or teacher, guide, such as Hadji Murat.

16. The first imam of Chechnya and Dagestan died in battle in 1832.

17. Sheikh Mansur Ushuma led the campaign against Russian incursions in the Caucasus for six years from 1785, but was captured and died in exile in 1793.

18. The so-called Decembrist rising of liberal officers in December 1825 follwed the death of Alexander I and was crushed by Nikolai, resulting in the imprisonment and exile of many participants. Among them was Zakhar Grigoryevich Chernyshov, whose considerable estate was coveted by his namesake, the future minister of war, at that time a prominent figure in the investigations into the conspiracy.

19. 'The Emperor?'

20. 'His Majesty has just returned.'

21. 'There's someone here.'

22. The widow of Nikolai's younger brother, Mikhail, who had died in 1849.

23. 'Poland and the Caucasus are Russia's two ulcers… We need at least a hundred thousand men in each of these territories.'

24. 'Poland, you say?'

25. 'Oh yes, it was Metternich's master-stroke to have left us with difficulties…'

26. In popular games of chance, such as faro, stakes could be multiplied by variously bending back the corners of cards and carrying bets forward.

27. A reference to the Biblical Joseph's relationship with Potiphar's wife.

28. Religious dissenters who continued to adhere to earlier ways long after the imposition of the reforms that caused the seventeenth-century schism in the Russian Orthodox Church.

BIOGRAPHICAL NOTE

Leo Tolstoy was born in Yasnaya Polyana in central Russia in 1828. The fourth of five children, Tolstoy was brought up by relatives after the untimely deaths of both his parents. In 1844 he embarked upon the study of oriental languages, then law, at Kazan University, but he never in fact took a degree. He instead returned to Yasnaya Polyana and, in 1851, accompanied by his eldest brother, he moved to the Caucasus where he joined an artillery regiment. It was around this time that he began his literary career, publishing the autobiographical trilogy: *Childhood* (1852), *Boyhood* (1854) and *Youth* (1857).

During the Crimean War, Tolstoy witnessed the siege of Sebastopol, before travelling widely throughout Europe. These two experiences had a considerable impact on him, and he became firmly convinced that the only way to change the world was to educate it. In Yasnaya Polyana he opened a school for peasant children. He married in 1862, and he and his wife (Sofya Andreyevna Behrs, who also acted as his secretary) went on to have thirteen children.

A voracious reader, Tolstoy was determined to understand the world around him. He then sought to explain his philosophical and religious beliefs through his fiction and against a backdrop of world events. *War and Peace* (1863–9), an epic tale set against the background of Napoleon's invasion of Russia, and *Anna Karenina* (1873–7), whose story of a young woman's tragic passion for an officer mirrors a universal quest for the meaning of life, are his two undisputed masterpieces. However, his later, more overtly philosophical works – including *A Confession* (1879–82) and *What I Believe* (1883) – were banned for their supposedly 'dangerous' views, and in 1901 he was excommunicated from the Russian Orthodox Church. Despite this, his writing continued to have considerable influence throughout Russia and beyond, perhaps most notably on Mahatma Gandhi.

By this time, Tolstoy had become seriously ill, and in 1910 he died at a remote railway station. His collected works, comprising some ninety volumes, were published in full between 1928 and 1958, and he remains one of the greatest prose writers of all time.

Hugh Aplin studied Russian at the University of East Anglia and Voronezh State University, and worked at the Universities of Leeds and St Andrews before taking up his post as Head of Russian at Westminster School, London. His previous translations include Anton Chekhov's *The Story of a Nobody*, Nikolai Gogol's *The Squabble* and Fyodor Dostoevsky's *Poor People*, all published by Hesperus Press.

HESPERUS PRESS – 100 PAGES

Hesperus Press, as suggested by the Latin motto, is committed to bringing near what is far – far both in space and time. Works written by the greatest authors, and unjustly neglected or simply little known in the English-speaking world, are made accessible through new translations and a completely fresh editorial approach. Through these short classic works, each little more than 100 pages in length, the reader will be introduced to the greatest writers from all times and all cultures.

For more information on Hesperus Press, please visit our website:
www.hesperuspress.com

ET REMOTISSIMA PROPE

SELECTED TITLES FROM HESPERUS PRESS

Gustave Flaubert *Memoirs of a Madman*
Alexander Pope *Scriblerus*
Ugo Foscolo *Last Letters of Jacopo Ortis*
Anton Chekhov *The Story of a Nobody*
Joseph von Eichendorff *Life of a Good-
for-nothing*
Mark Twain *The Diary of Adam and Eve*
Giovanni Boccaccio *Life of Dante*
Victor Hugo *The Last Day of a
Condemned Man*
Joseph Conrad *Heart of Darkness*
Edgar Allan Poe *Eureka*
Emile Zola *For a Night of Love*
Daniel Defoe *The King of Pirates*
Giacomo Leopardi *Thoughts*
Nikolai Gogol *The Squabble*
Franz Kafka *Metamorphosis*
Herman Melville *The Enchanted Isles*
Leonardo da Vinci *Prophecies*
Charles Baudelaire *On Wine and
Hashish*
William Makepeace Thackeray *Rebecca
and Rowena*
Wilkie Collins *Who Killed Zebedee?*
Théophile Gautier *The Jinx*
Charles Dickens *The Haunted House*
Luigi Pirandello *Loveless Love*
Fyodor Dostoevsky *Poor People*
E.T.A. Hoffmann *Mademoiselle de
Scudéri*
Henry James *In the Cage*
Francis Petrarch *My Secret Book*

André Gide *Theseus*
D.H. Lawrence *The Fox*
Percy Bysshe Shelley *Zastrozzi*
Marquis de Sade *Incest*
Oscar Wilde *The Portrait of Mr W.H.*
Giacomo Casanova *The Duel*
Friedrich von Schiller *The Ghost-seer*
Nathaniel Hawthorne *Rappaccini's
Daughter*
Pietro Aretino *The School of Whoredom*
Honoré de Balzac *Colonel Chabert*
Thomas Hardy *Fellow-Townsmen*
Arthur Conan Doyle *The Tragedy of
the Korosko*
Stendhal *Memoirs of an Egotist*
Katherine Mansfield *In a German
Pension*
Giovanni Verga *Life in the Country*
Ivan Turgenev *Faust*
Theodor Storm *The Lake of the Bees*
F. Scott Fitzgerald *The Rich Boy*
Dante Alighieri *New Life*
Guy de Maupassant *Butterball*
Charlotte Brontë *The Green Dwarf*
Elizabeth Gaskell *Lois the Witch*
Joris-Karl Huysmans *With the Flow*
George Eliot *Amos Barton*
Gabriele D'Annunzio *The Book of the
Virgins*
Heinrich von Kleist *The Marquise
of O–*
Alexander Pushkin *Dubrovsky*